Praise for the Base Branch Series

"Megan Mitcham's books are well-paced, well-plotted suspense novels edged with stunning sensual intensity. Her lovers are cold and deadly--except when they are skin-to-skin. I can't wait for the next book in the series!"

- **DELILAH DEVLIN**
New York Times and USA Today bestselling author

"Nail-biter all the way to the end."

- **Michelle**, MsRomanticReads
Adult Romance & Erotic Book Reviews

"This is a fresh and exciting story with lots of great characters."

- **5 Star Amazon Review**, Enemy Mine

"Megan now joins my elite team of must read authors. I fell in love with her work in *Enemy Mine*, and it just gets better the more I read."

- **TNT Reviews**

BOOKS BY MEGAN MITCHAM

BASE BRANCH NOVELS
ENEMY MINE
JUSTICE MINE
STRANGER MINE
WARRIOR MINE
DANGER MINE - July 2015
PRISONER MINE - January 2016
SURVIVOR MINE - April 2016

BUREAU NOVELS
FOR ALL TO SEE
PAINTED WALLS - October 2015

BLACKLIST SERIES
VERSIONS
VIRTUES - 2016

BOX SET
HEARTS IN DANGER - June 2015
benefiting The American Heart Association

ANTHOLOGIES
ANTICIPATION
CONQUESTS - 2015
ROGUE HEARTS - 2015
SEX OBJECTS - 2016
COWBOY HEAT
HIGH OCTANE HEROES
WILD AT HEART VOLUME II
benefiting Turpentine Creek Wildlife Refuge

Danger Mine

Base Branch Novel #5

Megan Mitcham

Copyright Warning

Published By MM Publishing LLC
Edited by Lacey Thacker
Cover Design by Deranged Doctor Design

Danger Mine
All Rights Are Reserved. Copyright 2015 by Megan Mitcham

First electronic publication: July 2015
First print publication: July 2015

Digital ISBN: 978-1-941899-13-7

Print ISBN: 978-1-941899-14-4

To my Brother Mine—the original title for this novel,

When Mom and Dad sat me down at the ripe old age of eight and told me I would no longer be the singular love of their lives I ran to my room, barred the door with my body, and told them you couldn't touch my toys. You ruined an awesome sleepover by barging into the world before the sun was good and shining. After waiting what seemed like forever with over half of our family in the waiting room, the doctor came and asked for me. He wanted to know if I was ready to meet my little brother.

I looked at your wrinkly face bundled in Mom's arms and, for the first time in my life, I fell in love. You weren't there to take love from me, but to multiply my own. Thank you for letting me be your second mother at times and your friend all the others. It has been a joy to watch you grow into a handsome and hardworking man.

I love you more than you'll ever know.

- Sis

Chapter One

Khani glared at the stacks of evidence and personnel files bloating her desk, the laptop that choked on its overflowing inbox, and a calendar stacked with meetings from before dawn until well past dusk. Her stomach rumbled, reminding her dinner had come and gone. She cleared another operative under the Eastern Headquarters of Base Branch Command from suspicion of treason with the scroll of her signature on another eighty-page report.

Thirteenth operative down. Only four more to go.

"Fuck you very much, Carmen Ruez."

The phone—hidden in the glut of her workspace—trilled. It snapped the last nerve in her overwrought system. Khani stood, snatched the receiver off the cradle, and then slammed it down.

The only person she wanted to talk to would call her cell. But damnit, he hadn't done so for two irritating days. Plus, all international emergencies funneled through her cell. Her fingers drummed the black plastic. She wouldn't call again. No use in it.

Her fingers wandered over the pre-set numbers to the directors of the UN, the CIA, the MI6, and all the other organizations that helped shape the political climate of the world. They danced across the extra long cord. Proven by her actions before she left London, her self-control had plummeted to earth, parachute be damned.

She hiked the receiver to her ear and dialed the same number she had twenty times today. Like every time before the call went straight to voicemail. Zeke's dark baritone and thick English accent filled the line. "Fuck off, unless you're my sister." Despite her mounting agitation over his lack of communication, a smile tickled the corners of her mouth. Like sister, like brother.

The message beeped. "Z, quit pouting and call me. I'm—"

A knock at her door halted the words. Unlike the main hallways of offices, Khani's office was nestled down a maze of corridors in a secluded corner of the floor. It suited her just fine. No one dropped by unannounced. Usually.

What she wouldn't give to have Rhonda, her and Vail's administrative assistant, back. The woman still had five more weeks of recovery from a gunshot wound she sustained on the premises two weeks ago.

"I'm getting worried," she continued. "And you know, I don't worry about much." Khani replaced the phone. She moved the bottom of the leather jacket she wore, revealing her side-arm. Bad guys usually didn't knock. She never did. But in light of recent events, cautious was better than dead. "Come in."

The woman responsible for every shit thing in Khani's life over the last month and a half sauntered into the office. Her petite curves undulated with every step. Carmen Ruez' brunette hair gathered at her nape in a low ponytail. The sun-kissed skin that added to the woman's Latin-goddess looks chalked around her cheeks. She looked like hell.

Sadistic satisfaction lightened Khani's mood. Though she had her reasons, it still made her a downright gobby person. "We're meeting on the range in ten minutes."

"I'm sorry to bother you. I tried to call, but it didn't connect." Carmen stopped at the black leather armchairs opposite the white lacquered desk. She gripped the top edge of the chair and inhaled. "I might not make it."

"You're here. You'll make it."

"Oh no." Carmen lunged for the rubbish bin.

Khani averted her gaze in time enough that she heard and didn't see the-bringer-of-bad-news toss the contents of her stomach in with the crumpled sticky notes and classified files that would be incinerated at the end of the day.

"Bloody hell, it's only a preliminary test. Not the final. It's nothing to get worked up over. I've scheduled others to test with you, so you won't feel pressured."

"So *I* won't feel pressured or *you* won't?" The woman's chin kicked up and she managed to look haughty on her knees hugging the trashcan.

"Pardon me?" Khani braced her hand on the butt of her new American-made 1911. When in Rome...

"I know you don't like me." Not a hint of her Latin upbringing curled her r's, even though anger thickened the woman's tone. Carmen wiped a hand over her mouth. A sapphire rock surrounded by glittering diamonds clung to her "it's official" finger.

"You breached the walls of a place sacred to me. You shot my commander. You ran him around long enough that a hit squad located your piece-of-shit brother in our state of the art facility, broke in, and nearly killed my co-worker. Your family turned one of our own against us. In the history of this organization, that's never happened. And you made me miss vacation with my brother, twice. So no, I really don't like you."

"If you're going to shoot me get it over with already, before I puke myself to death."

Khani slipped her hand from the now heated metal of her gun and straightened her jacket. "Sophie is the coolest chick I've ever met and she loves you. Vail has his moments and he loves you too. For them, I won't shoot you." She crossed her arms over her chest. "It doesn't mean we're going to be best friends. I won't forgive what you did any time soon. And I definitely won't forget it."

Carmen teetered. The arm not snuggling the bin shot out and strangled the ledge of Khani's desk. She heaved a breath. "Me neither. I don't know how Vail forgave me."

"Because he's a sappy love pup trapped in the body of a superhero."

The pretty Latina swung her head around, centering Khani in her pretty eyes. "Do you have a thing for him?"

"No." She managed to keep a straight face and mentally patted herself on the back.

"Shit." Carmen's body arched around the can again. Retching echoed out of the tin.

"Is Sophie sick?" Khani crossed the room, grabbed the towel from her workout bag and a bottle of water from the mini fridge.

Her long ponytail swooshed across her back with the shake of her head.

"Did you eat some crap from a street vendor?"

The ponytail danced again.

Khani scooted the leather chair next to her back. "Come on. Up. Up."

Carmen pushed off the floor and collapsed back into the chair with the puke bucket in hand. A whiff of acid hit Khani square in the jaw. Good thing bodily functions didn't rank on her give-a-shit scale. She just didn't want to clean it up.

"You know that's your rubbish bin now, don't you?"

A half laugh, half groan shook her torso. "If you did...like him, I could understand it. You work together. You—"

"He's a great guy, which makes him not my type." Khani thrust the towel and water at her. "Are you done yet or just warming up?"

"What is your type?"

"None of your business."

She set the glorified vomit bag on the other side of her and blotted her forehead with the terrycloth. "I think that's it, for now."

Khani's breath caught on the tip of her tongue. Her mind wandered down a tragic path for a split second. Was Vail's woman seriously sick? She couldn't be. He didn't deserve that. Carmen didn't deserve that either. No matter how much she'd screwed up on her path to freedom. "Are you sick, I mean really sick?"

A huge smile lit Carmen's face. Just like that, the pallor of death lifted from her cheeks. Her eyes misted over. "No. I'm not sick. It's no big deal. Really."

The alert honked on Khani's phone, telling her she needed to get to the shooting range. "Let me examine you. If you're running a fever, I'm not going to let you contaminate my guys. They're active and can't afford down time."

"I'm not feverish, but you can do your doctor thing if it makes you feel better."

"Damn right I can." She knelt in front of Carmen and held her hand out. "That's quite a ring."

"It's too much."

Khani pressed several of Carmen's bare fingernails. As soon as she released the pressure color poured back into the nail bed. She held the back of her hand to the woman's forehead. A clammy sheen clung around her hairline, but her cheeks gained pigment by the second. After a quick count on her pulse, Khani stood and flattened her slacks into place.

"If you're up to it, you're good to shoot. If not, we can reschedule for tomorrow." If she wasn't on a plane headed to the middle of no-f-ing-place to find her brother.

"Let me freshen up and I'll be ready. I know Vail really wants me to get through the preliminary qualifications so I can get to work."

"You aced the written exam last week and made it through the kill house like a beast. All you have left is PT and long-range accuracy. Then you'll be put with one of our best to train in the field."

Her eyes bugged. "The field? I thought I was qualifying for an office job."

"You are, but everyone in the office with the exception of admins and techs have been in the field. If you're ordering people on the ground you need to know what it's like to be face to face with the barrel of a gun, eye-to-eye with the bad guys. It makes for more efficient mission planners, intelligence distributers."

"Oh." Her gaze drifted into the distance, acclimating to the news.

"He just wants you to have something of your own, so you'll be happy with all the abrupt changes." Khani shrugged. "The loo is out my door and to the left."

Her gaze snapped back to the present. "I can't do this."

"Then we'll reschedule. It's not a big deal."

"No." Carmen sat the unopened bottle of water on the desk and shifted her knees toward Khani. She fidgeted for a second, and then wedged her palms between her clamped legs. "I mean I can't go into the field."

"I heard you were pretty bad ass. I don't think you'll have anything to worry about." Wow, Khani had said she wasn't going to be this woman's BFF, hadn't she? Yet here she was getting way too involved. Why, for the love of God?

Carmen grabbed the terry cloth from her lap and twisted the fabric to within an inch of its useful life.

"What is it, Carmen? Save us both the heartache and give. You know I'll get it out of you one way or the other."

That got her attention. The shoulders slumped in silent misery squared at Khani. Her wide gaze narrowed in challenge.

Sod it, she liked the lady's backbone. "What it is?"

"I'm late."

"As in...up the duff?"

"What the hell are you talking about?"

Khani tossed her arms into the air, giving vent to her dismay. Shit. To her way of thinking, this was worse than being terminally ill. "You know preggers, with child, totally shit-balls crazy you're having a baby?"

"Seriously looks that way with the morning and night pukefests."

"You don't know for sure? I mean, you haven't taken a test?"

"I've been a bit busy getting Sophie a wardrobe, registered for school, acclimated to a new city. Plus all my training hours." Her head bobbed in perfect choreography with her defense.

Air puffed out Khani's cheeks like a hot air balloon. Slowly she let them deflate. The girls had only been in the city for a two and a half, maybe three weeks now. Vail had been in New York for one of those reassuring the directors that Base Branch DC was secure in spite of evidence to the contrary. Of course they'd been holed up in a cabin in the middle of the woods for a while before that. Apparently there wasn't much in the way of entertainment. "Talk about fast work."

"I know." Carmen wilted against the chair back. "I can't believe it myself." Her gaze landed on her flat belly. The smile returned, but she pressed her lips together in a line. "Vail doesn't even know yet. I know he wanted this. I just don't know how he'll feel about it happening so fast."

"He'll be over the damn moon, and ban you from working in the field ever again."

"I can't say as I'm disappointed. I trained to do all that out of necessity, but I don't relish the life. I don't know how you do it all the time."

"It's the only thing that keeps me sane." Khani grabbed her cell phone off the desk and straightened. "Come on. You have a date with the shooting range, if for nothing else than for bragging rights."

"Bragging rights?" Carmen fell in step next to Khani with the puke bucket held away from them. Amazingly, the urge to strangle her had faded in the short time they'd spent getting chatty.

Khani held the door for Carmen. "V told me you picked off a quarter at sixty-nine meters, which means you'll hold your own with my guys. Not many people can do that and even fewer of them have boobs."

"I need to stop by the bathroom first."

"There's one on the way." She pointed at the bin, and then next to her door. "Just set that there. The cleaning crew will hate me, but they'll take care of it. Hell, they'll probably be thankful it isn't a body."

Carmen chuckled and relieved herself of the can. "You Brits and your sense of humor."

"I was being serious." Khani hooked a right and headed down the stairs to the basement. The other woman kept pace like she hadn't just tossed her guts. "When are you going to tell Vail? I'm pretty good at keeping secrets, but I don't want to keep things from him. Your relationship with him is based on trust, so is mine. I don't want to tell your news, but I won't lie to him either."

"He'll be back tomorrow. I'll take a test this evening and tell him tomorrow night." Carmen held the door at the sub-level of the high-rise. "I hope this won't put you guys in a bind. Vail made it seem like you really needed someone else to help out in command."

At the massive vault door, Khani allowed the computer to scan her retina. She entered her access code and swiped her access card. The door receded into the wall long enough for her and Carmen to enter the armory.

"He does. I'm in the field a lot, running my team. But I have someone else in mind for the job, had before you came along. I just have to track her down."

"That shouldn't be too hard for you."

"You'd think, wouldn't you, but some people don't want to be found." Khani nodded toward the bathroom. "We'll be on the range whenever you're ready."

"You're pretty nice for someone who doesn't even like me."

"Don't spread that around. It'd ruin my reputation. I'd have to smash you into the ground with my boot to earn it back."

"My lips are sealed." Carmen covered both hands over her mouth like the speak-no-evil monkey as she pushed the door open with her bottom.

When she disappeared around the corner Khani slipped her phone from her coat pocket and checked the screen. Nothing. She swallowed the disappointment and nearly gagged on the bitterness.

Khani aligned the bangs crowding her brow, stowed her phone, and continued through the armory to the range. The muffled boom of a single gunshot reverberated in the narrow space. A wall of pistols, rifles, earmuffs, and safety glasses decorated one half of the viewing room. On the other side a concrete buttress and ballistics resistant glass split the difference.

Warmth and comfort most people experienced when they stepped inside their homes cloaked her. Gun oil. The clink of brass hitting the ground. Sulfur and charcoal. The almost silent click of the trigger. It relaxed the knots at her shoulder blades. It eased the strain on her lungs.

Shit's bound to look up soon. Let it go and concentrate on the task at hand.

She snagged ear protection. A grimaced crinkled her nose as she wedged the thing over her hair.

"A beast like you worried about your hair? You think men care about misplaced locks? Not a chance. All we want are our broads bangin' and as far as possible from psycho."

Hunter stood in the range entrance. He waved both hands in the air and shook his head, indicating to the crazies to stay back. Each push defined a new plateau of muscle in his arms. Banded traps welled the collar of his graphite tee. "Can't handle that crazy shit. And that's the truth." A full-on purse stretched his thick midnight lips and added a whole new level of sexy to the man's game. His bulldog physique brushed either side of the frame.

"Your high expectations astound me. I thought tits and a hole to poke it in was all you boys required." Khani snickered.

"No, ma'am. Standards mean less headache later."

"He learned from experience." Oliver slipped his corded forearm around Hunter's throat, locked his palms together, and dragged him backward. Oli's blond man-bun flopped atop his head. His matching beard stayed put as though it were an extension of his distinct chin.

"Why don't you ever learn?" Hunter croaked.

"What can I say? I like an adventure." Oli huffed and struggled, fighting to keep Hunter from successfully wrapping his leg around Oli's and taking the fight to the floor.

Khani seized the opportunity and hurried through to the doorway. One mighty fine ass attached to hefty legs protruded from a stall halfway down the line. Scuffed cowboy boots crowned the feet. "At least one of you knows how to be serious...on occasion."

"Tyler, you kiss-ass," Oliver yelled.

Another rifle shot split the air, traveling at about twenty-eight-hundred feet per second. This close, the concussion of sound zipped through her veins. Like a plunger of adrenaline to the heart, hers kicked the beat from R & B to Dubstep. She headed for the control panel only a few feet from the door. "Prepare yourselves, children. I'm about to rock your world."

"Yes!" Hunter and Oli both barked the word.

"Yes!" She fist-pumped the air. "Moving targets at a mile."

Tyler rolled over and leapt from the ground, joining the other two in an advancing line of naysayers. They hovered a few feet away, having mastered their lesson in her personal space requirements.

Hunter spread his arms wide and hugged Tyler to his right shoulder and Oliver to his left. "Come on, LT. You can't do that for qualifiers. How could you stand to lose one of your Uh-Oh Oreos?" His wrists rested on the other men's shoulders and gestured wildly as they always did when he got excited. Which was all the time. "What's an Uh-Oh Oreo without an end, or the middle? Then it's just two white guys or a black guy and a white guy. None of those scenarios are as fun as an Uh-Oh Oreo."

The other two backed his ridiculous speech with nods and at-a-boys.

"Do I have your attention, gentlemen?" Khani asked.

"Yes, ma'am," Tyler said for the team. The guys snapped to attention, dropping their shenanigans for the moment.

"Good. In less than a minute Carmen Ruez will join us for her qualification test. I expect you to act like you work for the most well-trained covert operations organization in all the world as opposed to coked-out frat boys."

"We'll do you proud, LTC," Tyler announced.

"You always do. That's the only reason I put up with you wankers." Khani turned to the panel. "And you are testing at a mile, but it'll be a static target." She caught a glimpse of movement in her periphery. Carmen sashayed toward the door. "Also, be nice."

"Nice. You're asking us to be nice to the woman you promised to skin alive and wear as a coat?" Oliver's mouth gaped.

"The very one," she nodded.

The door swung open. Carmen stepped into the range with sure strides and fancy sound protection buds in her ears. And not one freaking hair out of place.

"Everyone find a stall, set up, and impress me." Stupid as it was, smug satisfaction curved the points of Khani's mouth. She liked giving orders, but having Carmen fall-in at her command cherried her sundae in a way very few things did.

She typed in the distances on their chosen lanes and set the timer. When everyone laid flat on their hips with an Accuracy International tucked under their chin she started the clock. The blare of a horn announced the beginning of the test.

As expected, no frenzy of movement erupted. Each shooter moved smoothly through the prescribed three shots, placing the brass cartridge into the barrel, sliding the bolt home, calibrating their sights, steadying their breaths, and then shooting.

In a window of four seconds the first and last shooters to finish stood behind their weapons with their hands behind their back. The concrete structure tunneled so far under the DC city streets that without a scope or binoculars Khani hardly made out the paper targets hanging approximately twenty city blocks away. She switched on the cameras at the end of the second, fourth, sixth, and eighth lanes and studied each set of shots. A sense of pride she had no right to feel since she hadn't trained these operatives, nor Carmen, to shoot, thumped her chest.

Her perverse brain flashed an altogether inappropriate image of the last operative she had trained to perfect a max of a one-inch spread on the mile shot—the clutch of her hands buried in King Street's bulging pectorals, nails sinking into skin. Sweat sheened their bodies. The phantom sensation of his heavy cock breaching the barrier of her taut body had her pulsing around a memory. The thrill of her driving thrusts plunging him deep inside her body gathered every drop of desire she'd banished to the corners of her psyche and crashed through her defenses.

The fingers she held over the keys shook. A single drop of sweat coasted across her belly. Her breath came in shallow pants as though she'd run to check the target and back to give her report, a report four people stood at her back to receive.

Fucking hell.

She inhaled a long drag of oxygen and used some of the same techniques the shooters used to calm their heartbeats to check her own. "I told you to impress me. And..." Khani erected the mask she used so often to hide her thoughts it was second nature, and then turned to the group. "You did."

Tyler bowed his head. Oliver and Hunter swayed their hips in an all too familiar victory dance. Carmen didn't move a muscle.

"Twelve shots within a two-inch spread. Individually, you sank them within the one-inch spread qualifier. Well done. Carmen, you can leave the gun and go. I need to speak with my team.

Gentlemen, collect your gear and meet me in the armory."

The brunette bowed her head and turned for the door. Her guys hit the deck and tended to their rifles. Khani stepped through the door with Carmen, let it close behind her, pulled off her ear protection, and fixed her hair as best she could. "Tell Sophie I said hello, please, and call me if you need anything?"

Carmen turned with an easy smile. "Thank you. You saved Vail. For that, I owe you everything."

The near black tips of Khani's hair tickled her neck as she nodded her understanding. Carmen left and Khani worked on composing herself further before confronted with the equivalent of a team of bloodhounds when it came to sniffing out weakness. Or arousal.

When would enough time pass that she wouldn't think about her stupid mistake and melt into a puddle of fuckable goo? Maybe never. Which was why she'd put an ocean between her and her biggest cock-up.

In a tidy line the men filed into the room with their rifles slung over their shoulders. Each took a side of the large counter in the center of the room. Khani flattened her palm on the cool black metal. Oliver stood to her left, Hunter across from her, and Tyler to her right.

"Ever heard the name Cara Ann Lee?" she asked.

All three shook their heads.

"She was a fresh CIA operative at the start of the Cold War. Beautiful. Cunning. Deadly. At twenty four, Cara almost single handedly brought down the iron curtain," Khani explained.

"Wait a minute," Hunter angled his head to the side and worked his jaw. "Did I read her name on a list of wanted ex-pats?"

"Probably. She's on there. Wanted for selling US intelligence to the Russians. There have been whispers that she's back in the States. I want you to find her. When you have, report back. Do not under any circumstances make contact. If she runs we'd have better luck digging for diamonds in my garden than finding her."

"You keep a garden?" Oliver's blue eyes plumped.

"Of course not. Across the pond a back yard is called a garden, but I don't even have one of those. Does that make my point even clearer?" she challenged.

"Yes, ma'am," Oli said.

"Is the goal apprehension?" Tyler asked.

"No. The goal is to have her join Base Branch command without bloodshed." Khani stuffed her hands in her pockets and watched the fireworks erupt. *WTF*'s snapped and crackled in the air before finally drifting into silence. "I've been called crazy before, but I would never do anything to jeopardize this operation. Its security is more valuable than my life."

Khani took a second to pin each of them with a quelling glare. "I have evidence that proves Cara was set up as a traitor and I have a good idea why. So, trust me and find her. Start with her daughter, Darinda Lee."

"Sorry to question you, LT," Hunter shook his head and gave a lopsided purse of his lips.

"Sorry, ma'am," Tyler agreed.

"We're assholes, LTC. Sorry," Oliver tapped the table with his balled knuckles.

"Clean your metal and get out of my sight." She turned toward the range.

"Want me to clean Carmen's gun?" Tyler asked.

Lip smacks and kissy sounds came from the other two.

"Nope. I'm in the field. I have to qualify too," she reminded.

A stampede of overgrown boys thundered behind her.

Oliver hurried past her and opened the door. "Hey, someone has to keep you honest."

"Three someones?" She arched a brow.

"Yes, ma'am," Tyler drawled. "Want a new target?" He headed for the control panel.

"No. This one will do." Khani walked to the farthest stall and eased onto her belly. She collected the spent casings, set them to the side, and lined up three new bullets.

"No shit!" Tyler whooped. "Carmen Ruez got the tightest spread."

"Damn." Hunter's word came from floor level. Khani tilted her head to the right. That big ass smile flashed at her from the far side of the small stall. Hunter rested his head on his fist. "Have to make sure you can work with distractions, LTC."

"Get any closer and I'll give you a distraction," Khani whispered.

"Understood, ma'am." Hunter smirked.

Khani blocked everything. The men. The irritation over Carmen. The arousal over a gaffe in her past. The worry for her brother. She snuggled the weapon, warming it with her body heat. The paper and its three close holes came into focus down the scope. She ticked the sight once. Twice. Her hips and the insides of her feet hugged the cold ground.

The buzzer blared.

She placed the cartridge into the barrel, slid the bolt home, checked her calibration, exhaled, and then fired. One. Repeated the sequence. Two. Repeated the sequence. Three shots.

"No fucking way!" Tyler enunciated each syllable.

"What!" Oliver dragged the word into a high-pitched whine of disbelief.

"What?" Hunter begged. "I can't see shit."

"Three shots. Three holes in the target," Tyler explained.

Khani sucked in a breath. She still had it.

Chapter Two

A man and woman with a brood spilled out the storefront of Sushi Capitol. Khani dodged an oncoming kid with a quick dip. Usually she called in her order, but with the flurry of activity before she left she hadn't had time. Hopefully, Minoru—the owner and Itamae—would take pity on a nightly customer—a starving one at that—and squeeze in her to-go order. She waited for the family to clear out, and then stepped into the little foyer.

The man she sought stood behind the tall bar at the back corner of the shallow space. Patrons cluttered the counter on high stools like well-mannered gulls awaiting the fisherman's catch of the day. Khani willed the quiet man to look her way, but his head stayed down. His hands moved efficiently over his workspace. His mouth held a concentrated line.

Every tiny table boasted coltish Hill staffers, save for the recently vacated four top, disgracing the honor of Minoru's nigiri masterpieces by leaving two yellowtail hunks behind. Bowls of soy sauce tinted green with gobs of wasabi added to the insult. The two-seater window bar around the foyer hosted one man hulking enough to take up both spaces. He wore a light jacket with the collar kicked up. The gold and maroon of a Redskins hat obscured his face further. His concealment and sheer size pinged her radar. Not to mention he didn't fit the customer mold, but then good sushi enticed all sorts.

Spring air wafted over her neck. Loath to have someone at her back that wasn't a Base Branch operative, Khani turned her back to the glass partition and the out-of-place man. A lawyer-type in a dark suit and loosened tie tripped on the tip of his dress shoe and stumbled his way inside. The chap's briefcase connected with her knee. Its impact created a nice *pop* in the narrow entryway.

Horror crinkled his face. "I'm such an idiot. I'm so sorry." He swiped the sweat off his brow and straightened. "I blame it on too many cups of coffee and too many hours of depositions. Are you okay?"

The impact hardly registered. "It's fine."

"You're not from around here, are you?" He didn't wait for her to answer. "Why don't you let me buy you dinner as an apology and you can tell me about what brought you to the States?"

This fella, though cute, didn't have the clearance or time for that long and twisted story. "I think you'll have trouble enough finding a spot on your own."

"Naw," he pointed over her shoulder. "The window bar is open."

Khani snapped her head around. Three twenty-dollar bills stuck out from beneath a large nigiri tray and not one spec of food cluttered the thing. She didn't consider the mound of wasabi to be food. She scanned the interior, but didn't find the man who knew how to eat sushi.

"There was a big man at the bar. Did you see where he went?"

"Nope. I was distracted by my clumsiness and a pretty Brit. So, what do you say, join me?"

"Thank you for the offer, but I'm just here to pick up my order. You go ahead and snag the window before someone else gets it." Behind him another staffer eyed the window seats, but waited outside the door for them to move.

"Fair enough. Sorry about your knee." The bloke bowed his head, and then dipped around the corner to the only two walk-in seats in the place.

The group outside the door swelled from one to three. A lone waitress hustled from table to table. Her cheeks flushed as though she'd been at it for a while. Khani groaned, and then sucked in a lung full of the aroma that kept her coming back here too many nights in a row. Her stomach gurgled. A masochist at heart, she stepped around the jutted corner to the front window bar to get out of the way and inhaled again.

She choked on the distinct scent of citrus, wood, and man. The couple holding hands while simultaneously gnashing bits of sashimi at the table three feet from the tip of her boot swung their gazes on her. But the cologne and the memories it brought with it gridlocked her attention.

Her gaze cut left and right. She'd been drunk on that scent many times, but had only partaken of its host one delicious day. None of the stick figures in suits had the height and bulk of a rugby player. Not one of them had the gaze that cut her through to the soul. But it couldn't be a coincidence that a chap of the same size and smell as Street haunted the restaurant she called dinner nearly every night of the week.

Oxygen knotted in her lungs. Her palms slicked. Every nerve in her body pulled her toward the back of the building, while her brain screamed for her to run out the front. One by one her sleek ankle boots treaded between the tables, past the crowded bar, and down the hallway.

Khani came face to face with an alarmed emergency only exit. The red handle screamed stop. She halted long enough to make certain the single water closet was empty, and then pushed through the door.

The alarm stayed silent. A thin metal strip covered the sensor on the frame.

No fucking way.

Down the narrow alley few lights illuminated business doorways. Night shrouded the corners. Ever cautious, Khani palmed her pistol and drew. She advanced on the first of two dumpsters. Her feet whispered across the asphalt. The closer she came to the corner the steadier her breathing became. This was what she did. Who she was.

She coiled, aimed, and then dipped into darkness.

An alley cat screeched loudly enough to rupture her eardrums. The thing shot down the backstreet as though she'd fired it out of her Wilson Combat. With her stealth blown to shit in a matter of seconds, she sprinted to the other dumpster, and then crouched behind it for cover.

Stillness enveloped the area. She held her position for several minutes. The longer she did the more doubt clouded her judgment. Perhaps her sanity had snapped and her psyche taunted her with the one thing she shouldn't want and couldn't have. She shook the notion away. A man King Street's size and smell had been in her restaurant tonight and snuck out the back door.

In full-on stealth mode, she eased around the corner, and then lunged into the line of fire—if someone had been crouched there with a gun. But no. The corner didn't even host a rat. She studied the alley one last time, feeling eyes on her though she couldn't see them.

Khani holstered her weapon. She kicked the dumpster. The loud *gong* whittled off enough of her agitation she could dial a phone number without smashing the device into the ground.

Why would her former operative be in the States and why would he shadow her? She had no clue, but vowed to find the answers. She dialed Law's cell and walked to the lit sidewalk while she waited the extra seconds it took to connect an international call.

"There are only a handful of people I'd be happy to hear from at this hour and I'm sleeping with one of them." Law's voice held none of the grogginess of one pulled from slumber, but years of round-the-clock training had honed the ability to function at a moment's notice. "Good thing you're on the short list."

"Bloody hell! I know there's a five-hour time difference between DC and London. I just forget that I'm not in London."

"You can do that? I mean, I haven't been there, but I hear Americans are quite unforgettable."

"Ignoring the obvious is my coping mechanism for homesickness."

"Come home. Then you won't be sick. Or surrounded by traitors."

As he did almost every time, he made reference to the former English colonials. Like he really cared. He just liked giving her a hard time. "Come on, wouldn't you fight for what you believe in? Don't you?"

"I'd stay and fight. Fighting with an ocean between your opponent is coward's work."

The comment smacked her across the face. Law hadn't been talking about her, had he? Intended or not, it applied.

"You didn't wake me to talk history. What's up?" Law asked.

"Have you heard from Zeke?" It wasn't the reason she'd called, but it should have been. She squeezed her nape and meandered with the flow of two old ladies back toward Sushi Capitol.

"Nope."

"He was supposed to be back two days ago and I haven't heard from him."

"Back from where?"

"Alaska."

"I though you two were taking that trip a couple of months ago. March wasn't it?"

"We were, but the thing with V happened."

"Oh yeah."

"Z was supposed to go without me, but he got called away for work and rescheduled. I thought it was going to iron out that we could go together, but then Rhonda got shot and we were put under the microscope. He left last week."

"How long was the trip?"

"A week."

"Hey, at least he won't freeze off his knob," Law chuckled.

"Frozen knobs?" Magdalena croaked. "Now that's bad news."

Law laughed harder. "Go back to sleep, love. All knobs are firmly intact."

"Oh, good," Mags said.

"Can we stop talking about knobs? I've been around them all day."

"You hussy."

"I wish. I'm not worried about Zeke freezing. I'm worried he might have been dinner for a grizzly fresh out of the den."

"I'd put my money on Zeke and light a barbecue for the bear. Khani, you know how he is. He'll turn up when he's good and ready."

Sure she knew Zeke vanished from time to time, but he always let her know—whether in an email or singing telegram—before he disappeared.

"Maybe he found peace in the great wilderness."

"Right. I find zen in make-up and shoes. Zeke finds it in big pints and even bigger women. We're city dwellers, Pierce. All of us."

"Then why the vacation to the last frontier?"

"Isn't the last frontier space?"

"That's the final frontier, if you're a Trekkie."

"Oh. Well, I missed him. I moved half the world away to be able to see him more than once a year, but it hasn't really worked out that way. I figured this trip would bond us or something."

"And then you didn't go. Maybe he's punishing you."

"It's possible. That's the only reason I haven't launched an all-out manhunt. Speaking of man-hunts, or women-hunts, have you heard anything about Cara Lee?"

"Last I heard she was causing a ruckus in your neck of the woods."

"If you hear anything concrete, let me know. How's work? Is the rookie holding his own?"

"Finally we get to it," Law sighed.

"Get to what?" she hedged.

"The real reason you called."

"Oh, stuff it, would you?" The old-blue-hairs shuffled along probably as fast as their brittle legs could carry them, but the stagnant pace only added to her annoyance. She banked left. A row of parking meters cut her off. The bastards.

"Not a chance," Law laughed. "And you can't call him a rookie anymore. The kid has more chops than most lifers. I really don't think he came to us straight out of college. He's too seasoned for that shit. You were commander before you left. Did his file say anything about prior training and for whom?"

"You're the commander now," she reminded.

"I *was* the interim commander. You know I didn't want the job. I hate paperwork. There was so damn much of it I hardly had time to eat, sleep, and bang my wife. Forget about snooping in files."

"Who's your replacement? When?"

"He wants to tell you himself. So, I can't say, but you'll approve. And it's been in the works for a month now, but you were dealing with some shit and he was getting jumped in, so to speak. Now back to Street's file."

"His file was sealed."

"No fuck?"

That tidbit—the reminder of it—revved Khani's over-stimulated brain. In her two years as commander of the London Branch office and one as lieutenant commander in DC she'd never come across another closed personnel file. When she'd called the UN director for her region asking questions about Street's background she'd met with a greased wall. Every attempt to maneuver around it or over it failed and she hadn't had enough time to devote herself to something so inconsequential. The UN had reasons for everything it did and it was all for the furthering of peace.

"No fuck," she finally sighed.

The white-haired ladies separated to pass an immovable object planted in the center of the sidewalk. King Street's hazy green gaze centered on hers, punctuating the futility of her fighting the attraction that had sparked the moment she first laid eyes on him. Her feet sank into the concrete as though it were quicksand.

"I've gotta go," she said into the phone.

"Good luck with it all. And hey, we always have a room or six, if you want to come visit."

Khani ended the call and shoved the phone into her pocket before her shaking hands dropped it. What the hell? In countless missions, dodging bullets and blades, covered in blood, hers and others, her hands never shook, no matter how steep the adrenaline drop afterward. She fisted them and crossed her arms over her thrashing heart.

Her lips suddenly seemed as dry as the cracked edge of the walkway. No way could she speak. Not that she knew what to say anyway. She dragged them into her mouth and whittled her gaze.

The jacket and hat no longer hid his features. What a shame for her heart health. He stood, relaxed, on his heels, as though he hadn't just parked a tank in front of an oncoming train. One hand pressed leisurely into his back pocket. The other hung at his side. Veins swollen, probably from his quick escape, contoured a forearm as wide as her thigh. An extra-large white T-shirt—she knew from experience—molded to every bulge and curve of his traps, pecs, and round shoulders.

His casual air, the one with which he interrupted her hard-fought center irritated her out of the momentary stupor. She tightened her fist in preparation to jab him on the square jaw or knock him upside his fat head. "Why are you here?"

The nostrils of his broken-many-times nose flared.

Khani salivated like a fucking dog in heat. She refused to swallow, unwilling to give him the satisfaction of knowing the effect he had on her.

"To buy you dinner," the Englishmen—who sounded more Irish than Brit—said.

His voice ratcheted her insanity to a whole new level. She hadn't heard it in months and it had been one of the things she found most appealing. His voice gave sound to his thoughts, which were often insightful. It was as if he'd lived four lives already and took the knowledge gained with him to the next. It had surprised the shit out of her at a time when not much stunned her.

She swallowed. Fuck him. "You've already eaten."

"But you haven't." He nodded in the direction of the restaurant.

"We don't have reservations and your window seats were taken."

"You needed a minute to adjust to the idea." One side of his mouth quirked.

"What idea?"

"The idea of seeing me again."

"Pompous ass."

"So, my being here doesn't bother you at all?"

"Why would it?"

"Great. Then let's eat. Don't worry. I'll get us a table." He turned toward Sushi Capitol and waited. He'd goaded her into that one. Yet another thing he did well—maneuvered people.

She'd mounted the ranks in a male dominated profession. She'd faced countless enemies and come out on top every time. She could share a meal with the man she'd let come inside her body. Couldn't she?

An inhale meant to fortify revealed just how shaky her nerves were. They rattled together like chains in a haunted house. One foot in front of the other. That's how she'd survived training and that's how she'd survive Street.

Khani stuffed her hands into her jacket, took a step, and then another. The smell she'd never been able to pin down caressed her cheek. Her steps sped, bringing her even with Street, and then propelling her past him. She didn't like anyone at her back, but it beat looking at him.

She grabbed the door handle and yanked it wide. In the time it had taken her to make an ass out of herself in the alley, talk to Law, and confront a man she never thought she'd see again, the crowd had eaten their fill and thinned. Street drew closer in the narrow foyer. She backed against the glass. Still his chest brushed her shoulder as he pushed past her and strolled to the waitress.

When the young woman's dark eyes lifted the two feet he towered over her petite frame her mouth literally dropped. The server nodded even before Street asked his question. Like she'd happily meet his every request.

An agitation altogether foreign settled under Khani's skin. She gnawed her lower lip. The powdery taste of cosmetics pricked her tongue. The new lipstick she'd bought—MAC's Lady Danger—probably stained the front of her teeth red and had her mouth looking like a well-used hooker's. She cut her gaze to the cooler of fish at the bar and ran her tongue along the front of her teeth.

"All set." Street pulled out a chair at a table against the wall. His open hand offered her to sit, while his expression offered nothing. "I ordered you a water, edamame, and a nigiri tray. Do you want anything else?"

"Yes." She pulled out the chair across from him and sat facing the street...both of them. Who the hell named their kid King Street?

"You are something else." He shook the crooked smile of his face and sat.

"I want to know how you know what I order," she demanded.

"I asked the waitress." Street pressed his elbows onto the table and held his palms together. The callused skin of his hand caused her own to dampen. His strong brow dipped. He looked at her with hooded eyes. "Anything else?"

"Why are you really here?"

He smiled for the first time. It held more mischief than humor. "I can't say."

"Or won't."

"Can't. You know how it is. Classified is classified." He whispered the last of it.

"Are you transferring?"

Street held her gaze for a full minute without moving or saying a word.

Oh, she played strong and silent with the best of them. Talking wasn't her strong suit anyway. She relaxed back into the chair and scrutinized him as closely as he studied her. Mystery shrouded this man and not in the I-wonder-what-his-hobbies-are kind of way.

Bloody hell. Mystery led to intrigue. With the way he fucked he didn't need to add to the temptation. She feared the answer would only pull her deeper under his spell.

The waitress brought two waters and steaming towels for their hands. She lingered by Street, and then collected his towel and finally hers. "I'll be right back with your appetizers."

The sounds of the low conversation, fidgeting, and mastication filled the silence of their table until the college student, or drop-out, returned. This time she carried two baskets of edamame along with her freshened face and now visible cleavage. Racist or not, Khani hadn't thought Asian chicks had cleavage. Apparently everyone did, but her. The waitress sat the food in front of each of them and batted her lashes toward Khani's dinner companion.

Khani straightened in her seat so quickly the young woman severed the string of drool she leaked over Street and looked at her. "You can leave now."

The waitress's mouth opened, but no words came out. Her eyes jumped from her to Street in rapid succession, before landing on Khani. She stepped backward. Her foot hit the chair at another table. The move must have bolstered her courage. She rebounded. "I didn't think you two were together."

Street leaned closer, his eyes intent and mouth curved.

Loath to answer the unspoken question for fear of pleasing either one of them with her answer, she planted her forearm on the table. Her hand crowned with a fist widened the waitress's eyes, but also screwed up the woman's mouth in defiance. Her long, board-straight hair fanned as she turned and stalked away.

Great. Now the little bird would spit on her food. Or worse.

She snapped her gaze to Street. "You enjoy that?"

"Immensely," he grinned.

Khani gawked at the food. "How much do you think I eat?" In the excitement, she forgot about her silence. Blast it.

"Not nearly as much as I do." He removed both baskets from the mound of green pods, and then plucked one from the bowl. His lips parted. The end of the husk disappeared into his mouth. He pulled the thing out slowly, dragging his lips over the skin as he had her skin too long ago.

Fuck it all.

In no mood for a demo of her oral skills— which he'd experienced firsthand— Khani popped the bean from her pods onto the plate before tossing them into her mouth. She'd only divested a handful of them when the waitress returned carrying two trays of nigiri and a pissy expression she directed at Khani.

Street cleared his decimated basket of edamame out of the way. The waitress moved to set a tray in front of him.

Khani scooted her basket over. "I'll take that one."

The woman's eyes narrowed. She looked from Khani to the tray and back.

"Yep, right here." Khani tapped the table.

Kimi—according to the nametag on her chest —slammed the tray in front of her, and then hesitated with the other one. "I'll be right back," she said to Street.

After the woman hustled away his shoulders shook with silent laughter. "How'd you know?"

"Please. This is literally child's play. I can't even believe I'm putting up with it. The real question is did you know and would you have let me eat it?"

"I had a feeling and no. If she tosses herself at every guy that walks through the door, there's no telling what you could catch."

"I doubt she throws herself at every one. Just the..." She clamped her lips together.

"Just the...what?"

"Just the fat-headed ones." She lobbed a soybean at his big head.

He caught the damn thing in his mouth and twitched his brow like the smug SOB he was. She groaned. His gaze locked on a place over her shoulder, and then shifted to hers, signaling that the waitress headed their way. A few seconds later the young woman breezed past.

Kimi stopped inches away from Street. She leaned forward, putting her tits in his face, and slid the tray with nine beautiful pieces of nigiri in front of him. Two cuts of fresh tuna laid over rice replaced the two strips of white fish that had occupied the tray. She slipped a piece of paper under one of its wooden feet. "Call me, if you want to have some fun."

The soybeans in Khani stomach fermented. She wouldn't give the little cunt or her one-time lover the benefit of seeing the display steal her appetite. Her fingers gripped the sticky vinegar rice and shoved the large piece of yellowtail into her mouth. With the fresh fish and rice combo doing crazy things to her tongue it didn't take long for her hunger to return. It also helped that Kimi was called away to deal with new Hillers in need of a table.

"This is so good," Street said two bites in.

She bobbed her head and finished another piece. "How'd you know I come here? Please don't tell me you've switched to stalker mode."

"Ask the right person the right questions and you can find out all kinds of information." He grinned, and then popped a hunk into his mouth as though it were no bigger than a bean.

"Law? No wait, Mags has a soft spot for you."

He shrugged and went palms up. "I can keep a secret."

That he could.

Street wiped his mouth with the napkin, leaned back, and folded his arms over his middle. The view incited her jangled nerves into a frenzy. Her jacket suddenly made a good insulator for baking her alive in the cool restaurant.

"Why'd you leave, Khani?"

The questions doused the flames and left a damp chill in her bones. She wanted to tell him to stuff it, that she wasn't his concern, but it would only prolong the inevitable. "I wanted to be closer to my brother."

"Since you've been here how many times have you seen him?"

Wow, that hurt, because the answer was not once since she'd moved halfway around the world to be closer to her brother had she actually laid eyes on him. And now he was MIA. "None of your damn business." She scrubbed her hands on the napkin from her lap.

"I want to know why you left."

"Sure I had other reasons. People usually do when making a big change. I was tired of riding a desk."

"Tired of riding a desk or riding me?"

Khani bit the sides of her cheeks to keep from speaking before thinking. She breathed deeply for several beats, and then relaxed. "It was one time."

"Three," he corrected.

"One day."

"I remember. Do you?" His Adam's apple rolled on a swallow.

"You think very highly of yourself, Street."

"Facts are facts. We fucked and you split."

"The fact is I have enough on my plate right now. I don't need you..." *Need you what? Screwing me? Screwing up my life?*

He ended the pause. "I never thought you did
__"

"Thanks for dinner." Khani stood and
dropped her napkin onto the table. "I'm sure our
waitress will happily provide your dessert."

She hurried to the door, and then darted
down the sidewalk as though guerrilla fighters
dogged her heals. Once safely inside her car and
zipping down the road, she called Zeke. Maybe she
should get him to carry out a hit on Street. This
time his voicemail picked-up without one hopeful
ring.

"Z, call me. Whenever. Whatever. Call."

Chapter Three

"Thanks for making the trip on such short notice." The commander of the Base Branch's eastern US headquarters stuck his hand out and squeezed Street's in a firm shake.

"Happy to help." He stepped into the office and sized-up the ace in a fraction of a second. Rough working man's hands. Stout frame. Intelligent eyes. Crooked nose of a fighter. In short, Vail Tucker was the warrior he'd heard tales about over the last two years of his Branch training.

Street closed the door behind him.

"You come highly recommended." Tucker stepped back and crossed his arms over his chest. An unexpected grin curved the side of his mouth. "I've never spoken to the Queen before, but she was adamant you were the man for the job."

"I can't believe she would break the silence to recommend me. It goes to show how much she trusts and values the Branch's work."

"No shit," Tucker laughed. "Now I know why your file was sealed."

"Her majesty's confidence is of the upmost importance." Street straightened to his full height to drive home his message. "If word ever leaked that she was behind the investigation, and subsequent public revelation, of decades of covered-up abuse that brought the Catholic church to its knees, it would rip England in two."

Tucker held his gaze. "She's a shrewd woman, recognizing your unique position, intelligence, and abilities, and then putting them to use."

Street harrumphed, the noise rattling his whole chest. "I guess it only makes me half a traitor."

"Not at all. It's all about the greater good."

Bitterness fringed his laugh. "While investigating, while serving my queen, I broke the trust of the only person on this pile of dirt that ever gave a shit about me. I dragged his demons into the light." Street scrubbed an itch on his forehead, and then drilled Tucker with his gaze. "Would you kill Carmen to protect innocents for things that are only possibilities and odds?"

The man's jaw flexed. His hands chaffed together. The dry friction released the tension in his face. "No. Which goes to show you're a better man than I am."

"That's an opinion not shared by many. Not even me."

"Then you're too hard on yourself."

"If I'm not, who will be?"

Tucker stepped around to the back of his desk and kicked back in his cushy leather seat. "Well, I know someone who will." He swiveled toward the phone, hit a few buttons, and the line trilled a half-ring.

"What?" came the gruff voice of his dreams.

"Good morning to you too, sunshine," Tucker said.

"I'm only on my second cup of coffee. The sun isn't up yet. I got shit for sleep last night. I have a

hell-a-lot of stuff to get done this morning, and
you're interrupting progress," Khani snapped.

"Give me ten minutes in my office. I'll lighten
your load," Tucker enticed.

"It's your funeral," she sighed.

"You saved me. You can't kill me. Besides, I
have fresh coffee—"

"I'm on my way." The line went dead.

"Have a seat," Tucker offered.

Street sank into the chair across from Tucker
and farthest from the doorway. When Khani came
into the office he didn't want to be in the direct line
of fire. He rested his elbow on the armrest and
scoured his hand over his chin. It wasn't the time
to smile, but damn. He hadn't had as much fun as
he'd had in the last twelve hours since he'd been
shot.

That sounded fucked up even in his own
mind.

Memories of that day enveloped his brain in a
fog of mystique and ecstasy. Khani's fingers glided
over the stitches he'd sewn into his own skin. His
arm throbbed, remembering the sting of her touch.
Other things throbbed too.

His forearms tingled from where she'd bound
him to the back frame of the wooden chair with
medical tape. His cock lengthened, remembering
her eager mouth working him deep, reliving the way
she stripped off her bottoms and straddled him
otherwise fully clothed.

"So," Tucker yanked him back to the present,
"you worked under Khani in London. I don't have to
tell you she'll be pissed at both of us for dropping
this on her with no warning."

"Nope, but I've dealt with her wrath before. I
quite enjoy the challenge."

"In a few days, remember you said that."

Tucker stood at the rapid click of a woman's shoes.

Street stood and braced for the bomb that was Khani Slaughter and the havoc she wreaked on his body and soul.

The door sailed open. "Where's the coff—" She stopped so quickly her onyx hair grazing the tops of her shoulder swooshed forward, momentarily covering her red mouth. Her smokey gaze bore a hole in his, leapt to Tucker's, and then back to him. Those long, lean, capable fingers whitened around her silver coffee thermos.

His pride evaporated. If Tucker wasn't in the room he might just fall to his knees and beg to get those hands on him again.

She stepped into the room and hummed the door closed. Boy was she pissed.

It had taken hours for her to let him kiss her that day. Once she started she hadn't stopped until she cut his bonds and rushed out the door. The experience taught him persistence paid off where Khani was concerned.

"It's good to see you again, LTC."

Chapter Four

Khani called upon every ounce of decorum she possessed and nodded at Street before slicing Vail with her gaze. "What's going on, Commander?"

Vail's mouth screwed into a knot. He hated when she called him that. She ticked a dash on her scorecard—which was behind quite a few points at the moment thanks to Carmen, her brother, Street, and now her commander.

"London Branch is lending us Lieutenant Commander Street to help clear us," Vail pointed between her and himself, "of all suspicion of traitorous activity for our part in the recent security breach."

That explained why Street wore a suit. She'd assumed he'd worn it only to inflame her lady bits. That might have been a better reason.

"Hold the fucking ringer." She stepped forward and smacked her empty cup onto the desk. Her gaze narrowed to slits on the horse-sized man who made the average desk chair look like a child's toy. "You mean to tell me, you're now LTC of the London office? How in the hell did that happen? I know five people off the tip of my nose more experienced than you, with more time in the outfit, and more..."

She thought to say mettle, but that wasn't exactly true. Street had taken a bullet saving three of their own from an ambush. A bullet that changed the course of her life.   He'd been off duty, put together the pieces of an intricate scheme on the open case, and acted without her clearance. If he'd taken the time to call for back up or get permission to act, the day would have ended more tragically than it had.

"No one was more surprised than me," Street said.

"Who appointed you?" she demanded.

"The commander," he answered smoothly.

"Who is..." She spread her arms wide, willing him to fill in the blank.

"He wants to tell you himself." One of his huge shoulders shrugged.

Khani snapped her gaze to Vail. "Do you know who the hell it is?"

Vail nodded his greying head once.

"And you're not going to tell me either. Un-fucking-believable." She slapped her hands together so hard it burned her palms. "And now he's here to clear us of suspicion. Well, he can start with you. I have to take some personal time."

The plush leather chair whined as Vail leaned forward and settled his elbows on his desk. "Street, will you give us a minute please?"

"He can stay." Khani ground both hands onto her hips and took a drag of oxygen. "This isn't about him. My brother is missing." Pressure built behind her eyebrows.

"Elaborate," Vail ordered.

"He went on an Alaskan adventure. When he got out of the wilderness he was supposed to call. That was two days ago. His phone is going straight to voicemail." The more she talked about it the tighter guilt hugged her.

"He's a capable man, Khani. Don't you think it's a little soon to worry?" Vail asked in an easy tone.

"If a team was due to report in at oh-two-hundred and they didn't, would you shut down your computer and call it a night?" She arched a brow, trying to work out the kinks and drive her question home.

"This isn't the same thing. He wasn't going on an op. He was going to whale watch and dog sled." Her commander shook his head almost imperceptibly.

"Sure it could be nothing, but if I know anyone, I know my brother." She pressed at the headache that gained strength like a pro athlete on the needle. "He wouldn't leave me hanging like this."

It might seem insane to Vail and Street that she'd jet set after such a short time. After all, she and Vail had tried on numerous occasions to hire him as a Branch agent. Her brother could take care of himself. He had since he was eighteen. Before that really. But he'd never broken a promise. Not to anyone. Especially her.

Vail lowered his twined fingers to the desk. "I trust your judgment. Where are you going and how can I help? We don't have many guys to spare right now, but Street can hold down the fort and I can give you a hand."

Nope. If Carmen was up the duff, V needed to be with her. "You can't go. Carmen needs you."

"What do you mean needs me?" His gaze narrowed. "Is there something I should now about?"

"She's great. But you just got back. Haven't even been home from the sound of it. She and

Sophie are in a new place. They deserve to have you around." She dropped her fingers from her forehead. They weren't doing a damn bit of good anyway.

"True enough," Vail agreed.

"I'll go," Street said.

A shadow cast over her shoulder. Since she'd stepped forward in an attempt to ignore his presence, the heat from his chest seeped through her blouse. Cold sweats chilled her skin and it took every bit of her training to rein in what might have been a full-blown panic attack or a dead body on V's floor.

Khani whipped around, putting her back to the wall. Street stood like he was ready to hit the tarmac within the minute.

"No." Khani's excessive volume echoed in the utilitarian space. She despised her telling retreat and automatic refusal. "I need you to finish those reports and get them to New York, otherwise none of us will have a job." Her headache twirled her optic nerve into a tangle of pain.

She turned to Vail. "I just need some cold weather gear and Street to finish my operative reports."

Chapter Five

It took some fancy footwork, but Street got what he needed from Tucker. Just like he did from everyone. Almost everyone. Reading people's cues—those minuscule ticks of a facial muscle, near imperceptible shifts in their gazes, the beat of their pulse—gave him the edge essential to his survival.

Street didn't need any special skills to discern that the wall of muscles and attitude walking his way down the basement corridor were three Base Branch operatives agitated by his presence in their inner sanctum. Couldn't say as he'd blame them considering the mess they'd been in a couple of weeks ago.

Man-bun's hand flew to his sidearm the moment his blue gaze lit on Street. The black guy hulked out. The already pronounced muscles defined by his tight shirt rippled as he prepared for battle.

The tallest of the three, hitting eye level with Street thanks to the boots on his feet, narrowed his gaze. His grip doubled on the file in his hands, bowing it to hell and back. "Your call-sign, now," he demanded.

"Sure," Street smiled, "if you can beat it out of me." He wanted to see how they'd take him in a narrow hallway with no cover.

Three big men scattered. The two white guys moved to the wall and drew on him, while the guy in the middle barreled up the centerline.

Street slowly put his hands in the air. "I'm just tuggin' your balls. Juliett. Oscar. Hotel. November. Sierra. Mike. India. Tango. Hotel. Zero. Zero. Zero. Zero."

The thunder rolling at him stopped with a clap of boots two feet from the tip of the black wingtips that complimented his monkey suit. At least, that's what the sales lady had told him. But high-dollar clothes were one of the few things he knew jack about.

"I heard you were big and crazy as a broke-neck chicken," the cowboy called. "Now I know it's true."

"You're the one who took down Aldo Bassani? I heard the guy was like a ninja." Intelligent brown eyes studied Street from head to toe. "You're a toe-to-toe heavy-hitter type."

"Goes to show you shouldn't believe everything you hear. Though, they aced the loony part." Street shrugged. "Now, can I pass? Or do you fancy a round or two?"

"We're cool. I'm Hunter." The stout man presented his fist.

"Street." He tapped knuckles with the bloke's.

"That's Oliver and Tyler," he explained.

He nodded to each of the men. "You come from the armory?"

"Yep." Tyler stowed his gun. "You need in?"

"Na, I've got the code, card, and my blinker is in the system." Street winked. "I'm just looking for Slaughter. Have you seen her?"

"So, are you the reason she's in a shit mood? If you are, I'm not sure I'm ready to put down my weapon." Oliver scowled.

"I tend to have that effect on her, yes." Street
pushed a hand into his pocket and tapped the
center of his chest with the other. "Here you go."

"Damn it." Oliver holstered his gun. "You
have to tell me how you do it. We've tried everything
to light her up." He pointed back and forth between
him and Hunter. "Nothing works. She's always so
mellow, but not today."

At least he affected her in some way. That
knowledge made his trip worth the trouble of
convincing the queen of England to do him a proper
and recommend him for the job.

"It's just a gift." Street shucked his suit coat.
"If you'll excuse me, I have a date with destiny."

"Yeah, if your destiny is about four square
yards of dirt," Oliver laughed.

"Meters for me." Street stepped past the men
and then turned around. "All of our destinies are
dirt, unless you get cremated."

"You Brits have one hell of a dark sense of
humor," Tyler twanged.

"It's the fog." Street strangled his jacket in
one hand and yanked on the tie with his other. "You
blokes be safe."

"Always." Hunter bowed his head and then
the lot of them headed down the corridor.

Street turned the corner, braced himself to
see Khani again, and then jumped through the
ridiculous series of hoops it took to get inside the
vault. The door slid open. Her blustery gaze hit him
full-on. Both her hands braced on an island in the
center of the room. A pen bowed her middle finger,
holding it against the back of her others. She stood
on the far side with her back to the wall like she
always did.

A laptop sat to her left. She hunched over a
map spread across the table. Three bags, rope, a

tent roll, headlamps, knives, MRE's, and other gear littered the bench to her right.

He stepped into the room and her expression hardened. "V already gave you a key to the place, huh?"

"You're really going after your brother." He'd thought her withdrawal from duty, no matter how brief, was a result of his presence. What a whopper he was. She didn't give two shits about him. When would he ever get that through his soft skull?

She huffed. "I can't sit around and wait to find out he froze to death on a trip I pushed him to go on, a trip..." Her slightly uneven front teeth bit her lower lip, stalling her sentence as though she'd said too much.

"A trip..?"

Khani slammed the pen onto the table. "A trip I was supposed to go on with him."

"You would've if you could've."

"You don't know that." She pushed the heel of her hand at her brow and spat the words like venom.

"Yeah, I do," he argued.

"Just because you've been inside me doesn't mean you know me."

"Not for lack of desire." Street took a step forward, and then another. He tossed his coat onto the black counter. Khani's backbone went arrow straight. She'd break her own spine before she'd back down from anything.

His heart did flips like a bloody schoolgirl. This lass made him such a sap. He couldn't bring himself to care. "I'm going to help your headache." He rounded the counter. His shoes stopped inches from hers. He raised his hands slowly toward her throat.

The crack of her palms on the back of his hands reverberated through the room and traveled up his arms. "You just want to cop a feel."

"Not denying it, but this is strictly homeopathic." He tried again.

"I'm a licensed nurse." She wrapped her hands around his wrists—as much as they would fit—and shoved his hands way.

Street let his gaze sink into the tempest of hers. He swallowed against the dryness of his throat. Blimey hell, she flipped him on his ear and had him scrambling to find which way was up. He licked his lips. "I would never hurt you."

She grumbled something under her breath akin to, 'bullshit' or 'too late.' Her hands balled into fists, and then dropped to her sides. "If you really think you can make it stop, give it a whirl. But stay in front of me."

It must have been one hell of a migraine for her to agree to let him touch her. His fingers hadn't had the pleasure, not even when he was buried to the balls inside her. Street filled his constricting lungs with her scent. He wrapped his right hand around the column of her neck.

Her eyelids raised and her breath caught. The pulse of her carotid battered his fingers.

"Breathe." He braced his thumb and middle finger on either side of her jaw. His other hand slipped underneath her hair. The heat of her body warmed him from the outside in. A knot of muscles greeted his touch. "For this to work, you're going to have to relax."

Khani's eyes rolled into the back of her head. Sadly, it had nothing to do with ecstasy and everything to do with irritation. She blew out a breath. The moist air caressed his neck much like it did when she rode him to the brink.

His cock grew, testing the bounds of his trousers. He ignored it. Hell, he really tried. He massaged her sub-occipital muscles, rubbing each one from the base of her skull to her nape.

Degree by hard-won degree, Khani's shoulders slackened.

Street kept his gaze locked on hers. He pressed from the front and pulled from the back. The harder he dug into the muscles the more limber she became in his grasp. Her rigid form no longer limited his ability to mold her to him with his touch. Optimism he had no right to feel bubbled inside his mind and solidified his purpose for coming.

He'd push her. Not too hard or too fast. But no matter how hard she shoved him back, he refused to give up on her.

Under his prodding fingers the knots worked out of her muscles. He smoothed the length of her nape from skull to back one last time, and then removed his hands from her skin. But not his gaze.

She waggled her brows. "How'd you know to do that?"

"I had an interesting upbringing. Learned a thing or two along the way to save money."

"Save money? You have a flat screen as big as a bus hanging in your flat."

"It's my first telly and I worked hard to earn it." He stepped back. "And so we're clear, I wouldn't presume to know you. I'd like to know you, but it would take some extraordinary circumstances for you to allow that to happen."

She turned toward the computer. Though he was denied the connection of her gaze, he was gifted with the profile of her fit body. Her small breasts curved delicately in the gauzy material of her shirt. Tight-legged black trousers hugged every inch of her lush bottom and accentuated the grace of her long legs.

"I don't do relationships." Her finger tapped on the keys. A topographical view of the same map appeared on the screen.

"You're friends with Law and Magdalena. Why not me?"

"You're confusing banging with friendship."

"Am I?"

"You want to be my friend?" She peered over her shoulder, her eye drawn.

"Yes, I'd like to be a friend to you."

"Why?"

"I've asked myself that a few thousand times. When I come up with an answer I'll let you know." True talk, he'd spent more time thinking about Khani than he should spend thinking about any problem except how to end world hunger, create lasting peace, fix the foster care system, or reverse global warming.

Bangs hung almost into her eyes, covering her forehead. Artful, but heavy black, liner rimmed her ashen eyes, amplifying their gloom. A shellac very similar to her porcelain skin tone camouflaged her cheeks along with a burst of color that offset the sharp red mouth she'd painted on. And then it struck him. Her make-up acted as a shield.

Khani clasped her upper arms, hugging herself. She stared at him as though he were one of those big problems she needed to solve. "The people I fuck and the people I'm friends with don't overlap. Life is complicated enough without adding to the drama."

"You handle complicated beautifully. I've seen it."

"On the job," she corrected with a flip of her fingers. "My personal life is off limits. Besides, you don't seem like the relationship type either."

"I'm not."

"People don't change, no matter how much we want them to." She blinked three times in a row, which was more rapid than he'd ever seen her calculated eyes move.

His gut twisted. Somewhere along the way someone had hurt her. Badly. He'd sensed it all along, but now he knew for sure. He just didn't know who, when, or how. But he would.

Surprisingly, she turned her back on him and clacked away on the computer. That in itself was a victory of sorts. Small-won battles turned the tide of wars.

He took one calculated step forward. "It's easy for people to dismiss others, to say they don't change. But if a person wants to, they can change."

She stilled. "If I wanted to, I couldn't give you what you're looking for."

"You sell us both short, but that can change too." He left the room and took his small win with him. He'd have to accumulate a lot more before she'd take him seriously.

Chapter Six

Was there anything more irritating than a commercial flight? Khani gritted her teeth and shuffled forward in line. King Street was more irritating, but he wasn't present. The horde of misfits cramming into the belly of the plane like sardines eager to be vacuumed into the can together started edging out the competition.

Khani held her carry-on high enough that she didn't thump every head lining the aisle. She clamped her left elbow over the pistol dangling from her shoulder holster hidden beneath her leather jacket. If one passenger got a peep of the handle they'd work the crowd into hysterics and delay the flight...even more than the forty minutes they'd already wasted due to the plane's late arrival.

She waited, shuffled, and then waited more. The spiked heels of her boots dug into her foot. There hadn't been time to go to her condo and change. Luckily she always carried a bag of clothes in the trunk of her car, but she might need all of them for the days away. So, she shifted her weight from one foot to the other and worked her way to the very last row.

A salt-and-pepper headed chap—around her dad's age—rested his head against the back of the seat. His loafer-laced feet stuck out into the aisle.

His hands were clasped on his trim belly while one finger tapped the expensive watch on is wrist. She bet he was wondering where the hell the first-class seats had gone too. She'd certainly have ponied up the extra dough for some elbow room.

"Excuse me." Khani shoved her bag into the compartment overhead.

The man blinked her into focus. "Well, you don't need an excuse, beautiful." Whiskey curled off his breath and stung her eyes.

Perfect.

"No, I don't. I need you to get up so I can take my seat."

"Oh." His shifty brown eyes assessed her, legs to boobs, boobs to legs, and then back again for good measure. "I'll let you crawl over." A fat tongue lolled from his mouth and lapped over his lips.

"And I'll give you one more opportunity to move."

"Or what?" he snickered.

Khani slammed the lid to the overhead compartment closed at the same time she rammed her boot heel into the top of his shoe. "Oh blast, I'm sorry. I didn't see your foot there."

The man's face marbled into hues of red. He bolted upright in his seat. His cheeks puffed.

"Would you like me to crawl over you? Because I think I'd quite enjoy that." She flashed her brightest smile.

He slurred a string of curses under his breath, but stood, and then hobbled out of the way.

"You're too kind. Thank you." Khani shifted into the narrow space. She collapsed onto the seat. The stiff seat back cradled her enough that sleep would find her after take-off. This was likely the only down time she'd have for a while and she'd learned early on to take it where she could get it.

The man flung himself into the seat. It shuddered under his petulant display. She ignored him and watched the men in orange vests toss luggage from one cart onto another. The cache of weapons and ammunition in her bag assured no one would be playing catch with her duffels.

Silver linings.

"I'll trade you this seat for a front-rower with tons of leg room and no foot traffic." The all too familiar baritone hawked his c's and rolled his r's.

Khani turned, not believing her ears. Every muscle in her body constricted. King Street's height and breath gobbled all the available space in the aisle and more. He tilted his head to the side and winked.

A tingle washed over her skin, just like it had in the armory when his hot hands touched her.

"Absolutely. She's nuts." The chap used the chair in front of him to stand.

"A2." Street got as small as a big-ass man could in the limited room of an airplane aisle and let the bloke shuffle past. Street adjusted his fancy jacket, smoothed his tie, and then eased into the seat. "It's too bloody hot for coats."

"I didn't think you owned one. I'd only seen you in jeans and T-shirts until today."

"Nah." He hooked a finger into his collar and tugged at the material. "That's not true is it? You've seen me in far less." His head remained facing forward, but his gaze slid to her.

The tingle heated into a sticky mess of hormones that threatened to melt her resolve on the matter of Street. She pushed the palms of her hands onto the tops of her slacks. "Why are you here?"

"Why aren't you using the Branch jet? Commercial flights blow."

"I would have, if I could have, and I'd have made certain the captain took off before you stowed away."

His beautiful cheeks balled into a grin. "It's all about the sweet nothings you whisper in my ear."

"My team needed the jet to check some leads. The chopper wouldn't make the distance. The C-17 seemed like over kill for just me. Why are you here?" She needed him to turn so he'd see her outrage at his constant bulldozing of her life over the last twenty hours.

"Vail sent me to Anchorage, Alaska." His greenish-brownish-blue eyes rained on her with the singular intensity of only the best Branch operatives.

She wished that gaze closer and farther at the same time. "He knows better."

"I don't take orders well," he shrugged.

"As I recall, you take them very well."

Why in the bloody fucking fiery pits of hell had she said that?

"Only from you."

She'd gone to stitch him up and read him the riot act about making a move solo. But she'd really gone because she needed to see that he was okay. The moment she'd laid a hand on him her self-control vanished. And she controlled him instead.

He surrendered himself completely. The beauty of it, the simplicity of it had frightened her right out of England.

Khani tore her gaze from his and searched for the vested men, the luggage, anything to get her mind off Street's large body so close to hers, so within reach. The engine rumbled to life, drowning out the sharpest screams of her desire. Slowly they rolled away from the gate and toward the runway.

Her sleep plans parachuted off the plane, fell ten feet to the tarmac, and went splat. No way would her pulse calm enough to even relax into the seat.

The aircraft barreled into the sky and she continued staring out of the window as the world shrank, shoving her closer to Street then she ever expected to be after she left home. One minute down. Two hours and forty-six minutes to go. Thank goodness he knew when to shut his mouth.

In an effort to maintain her sanity, Khani forced her mind away from Street and onto her goal. Find Zeke. Sure he'd vanished for weeks, months at a time, but he always warned her before he left. If he ever told her he'd call or meet her someplace, he did. No exceptions. She stared at the patchwork fields, and then the blank ceiling of clouds, and wondered what the hell had happened to him.

"Pretzels or peanuts?" a saucy voice asked.

How had she missed the ever entertaining this-is-how-we-make-you-feel-like-you-have-a-fighting-chance-if-we-crash directives and the beginning of cabin service? They were the highlights of any commercial flight. That and watching drunk people get dragged off the airbus.

"Yes," Street smiled. Either he didn't know it was an either-or question or didn't care.

"It looks like you need my whole stash or a steak and baked potato." The redhead with boobs up to her chin offered a handful of peanut and pretzel packs.

"I can always go for a steak." His wide hand rubbed over his flat abdomen.

Khani couldn't take the time to evaluate the move on a scale of sexy because the attendant's pupils dilated.

"I bet you can go for lots of things." Ashley—
the nametag on her ta-tas gave her away—leaned
in, leading with the money-makers.

"For the love." Khani couldn't help herself.
"Have some respect."

"Oh God." One of Ashley's hands flew to her
bosom. "I didn't know you two were together. I'm so
sorry."

"We're not." Khani sighed. "I mean," she
whispered, "have some respect for yourself. You
don't know his first name and you're ready to throw
down in the bathroom."

Ashley's pouty mouth gaped like a fish
seizing its last breaths. She spun on her heels and
dashed up the aisle.

Street swiveled his head at Khani. "Way to go.
No peanuts or pretzels for you."

"Shut it." She folded her arms over her
middle and stewed. Why had she said anything?
Street's shenanigans and Ashley's quick-draw
weren't her concern. "You aren't going to share?
You have about ten packs of each."

"I'm a growing boy." His shoulders twitched.

"Yeah, growing fat in the head."

His Adam's apple bobbed on a quiet laugh.
"It's your fault. You keep defending my honor."

He had a point. She was like jello around
him, incapable of controlling herself. She'd have to
ditch him. They changed planes in Minneapolis.
She could pull it off there. She'd researched a
private airfield fifteen minutes from the airport as a
contingency.

King Street counted as one huge unseen
probability. She hated abandoning the gear she'd
checked, but she could buy more in Anchorage.
She'd just be out the long-range rifles, which she
hoped were overkill anyway.

"Here." He held out two packs of peanuts and two of pretzels. "If you don't eat them now, stow them for later."

Those seemingly simple words combined with his earlier comments about his television and saving money tugged at her heart. Since his file had been sealed she didn't know what kind of childhood he'd had...other than interesting. That's what he'd called it.

She wanted to know about his early years, but refused to ask. The problem was when you asked someone questions they assumed the road went two ways. And she didn't talk about her past. It was firmly behind her. She kept it there and smashed the rearview.

Khani knew hungry. Once you were truly hungry you were always hungry. There were protein bars in her glove box, desk drawer, gym bag, the dresser beside her bed, and in almost every room in her condo. She hardly ever used them, but they were there. And more, she didn't waste food. Had Street ever known real hunger? She hoped not.

"I will," she croaked. The packages crinkled as she stuffed all but one into her pocket. She opened the small, knotted pretzels even though her stomach resembled one and crunched a few. "I guess I screwed us both on water."

"That you did." He gave her that sideways glance again.

"Sorry." That look made it as hard to swallow as the dry dough in her mouth.

"Luckily I came prepared for your shenanigans." He pulled a small bottle of water from inside his jacket.

"How can you fit that in your jacket?"

"Big guy. Big Jacket. Big..."

"Dick," she finished, giggling in spite of herself.

A chuckle erupted from the seat in front of them.

"That too." He grinned. "But I was going to say, pockets."

"Of course you were." She took the bottle from his grasp, pulled two swallows, and then handed it back. "Thank you."

"Thank you?" A furrow developed between his brows. "I expected a bigger fight."

"How am I going to fight? There's nowhere to go."

"I wouldn't have put it past you to pull the emergency exit and use your jacket as a parachute."

"There are kids on the plane. Can't freak them out."

"That's mighty nice of you."

"What can I say, I'm a nice girl."

He leaned back into the chair and canted his head. "You are. No matter how bad-ass, you have a soft spot."

"Sharks have soft spots too. But the people who feel it don't long survive the teeth."

"I'm tougher than I look." Street leaned forward. His hands moved slowly, but purposefully over her lap. He grabbed the ends of her lap belt, and then clicked them together. "We've started our decent."

"And you think this will save us in a crash?" she whispered.

"It can't hurt. Can it?"

There were too many meanings to that question and in his eyes to answer. She grabbed her resolve to flee with both hands and hung on until they hit the gate. They hurried through the tunnel. Having wasted thirty minutes getting off the plane, there were ten left to make it to their connection five gates away.

She headed for the bathroom. "I have to pee. You?"

"I'm straight."

"Oh, I know that."

He studied her down the end of his nose. "I don't have to pee."

"Okay, will you grab me a water and a protein bar from that little store. Do you want to meet there or at the gate?"

"The gate'll do."

"Great. Thanks." She hurried across the wide thoroughfare, dodging strollers, ambling teens, and old people.

Khani slipped into the bathroom and locked herself in the first stall. Her bag hit the floor with a *thunk*. Both hands blew through her hair, yanking it to the top of her head. She yanked a beanie from the bag's side pocket and pulled the olive hat low over her eye-catching hair. Next came her jacket and holster. She pealed them off and shoved them into the duffel.

That should be enough to get her out of the airport without catching his eye. She plucked the bag off the floor and headed for the exit. The terminal hummed with activity, which worked in her favor. Without a parting glance she headed right out of the bathroom, away from the store, the gate, and Street. Those were the things that got a person caught. Sentiment.

Her heels tapped a rapid staccato on the tile that matched the beat of the business travelers she melded into. Past the first gate her stride held, but a tiny bit of the tension seeped from her shoulders.

It would cost her a hell of a lot of money, but it was worth it to get away from Street.

She dragged in a heavy breath and released it.

The group she moved with parted quickly and she met the man that haunted her dreams...and now waking hours. He'd lost the tie, two buttons at his wide neck, and turned up his sleeves, revealing his daunting forearms.

"It'll take more than a hat and a change of top to mask the sway of your hips, Khani."

"Damn you." She shoved at his pecs. "I don't sway my hips."

"Nope. But they sway in spite of you. Mighty nicely too. Now, let's go before we miss the flight and actually have to charter a flight."

"Just let me go on my own. You're only making this harder on both of us."

"I don't like easy. It's boring."

Chapter Seven

She gave him the silent treatment, which he had to admit she did better at this time around. Two hours in and not a word. They'd managed to wrangle the emergency exit seats. It afforded them more leg room, but Khani hunched into a ball of rage. Too bad for her, he found her pouting pretty damn cute.

He might be sealing the nails on his coffin, but there were some things he needed to know before they landed. "Tell me about your brother."

"Why? Did you run through the entirety of the female persuasion?" Her head snapped around so fast, her hair flipped out at the side. "Are you moving on to fresh territory?"

"Oh, I tried fucking you out of my system." He *tsk*ed. "Didn't work."

"Lucky me."

"Your brother?"

"Isn't your concern."

"You guys are close." He confidently stated the fact. You didn't shirk your job to trounce about the wilderness for someone you don't care about.

She screwed up her mouth. Her savage gaze narrowed in challenge.

"I'll find out one way or the other. I won't go into a situation blind. I'd rather you tell me though."

Khani didn't say another word until she cursed into her phone while he procured them a rental at Anchorage International Airport.

"What?" he asked, though he didn't expect anything more than a curse directed his way.

"The tour company is closed."

"I'd guess as much. It's what…9 p.m. They've probably been closed for four or more hours."

"Thanks, smart-ass. I know that. I just expected them to have a recording with their hours of operation at least and a report about delays or weather bulletins at most."

"Here are your keys, sir." The woman slid keys and a slip of paper with a handwritten number scrawled across it. "If there's anything you need. You know … if you have questions about the vehicle, need roadside assistance, or anything, here's my number."

"Thanks really, but I think I can manage." He scooped up the keys and headed for the lot before Khani lit into another friendly woman. Not that he wouldn't enjoy seeing her claws, but they had more important things to handle. Her lack of trust in him and all of non-brother mankind, for starters.

"You want to drive?" he asked over his shoulder.

"You'd let me drive?"

"You like control. I can appreciate that."

Her lips pursed as though she had difficulty reconciling his meaning. "Wow," she breathed. "You drive. I'll navigate."

"That works." He popped the hatch and deposited the three large bags he carried inside.

"You want your carry-on back here or up there with you?"

"Up here. I have some files and info I need."

"And your gun."

She hitched a brow, and then nodded.

He shut the gate and hopped into the SUV. "Where to?"

"The tour company. A left once we get out of the lot."

Street pulled the vehicle out of the parking garage and swerved through the loop-d-loop of arrival and departure lanes. "You said they're closed, right?"

"Yes, but I don't need anyone working there to get in and find the information I need."

"We." He turned left onto the road and clicked on the heat and rear defrost. It was May, but May in Alaska frosted his man nipples.

"We what?"

"We are doing this together. You need to get that in your head. I know you can work with others. You wouldn't have gotten this far in the Branch office without the skill. You need to engage it."

"Yes, sir." She tucked one foot into the seat and wedged it under her thigh. The longer they drove the taller the buildings grew. Soon they coursed through Anchorage's pulmonary artery. "Can *we* take a left at the next road?"

"Now who's the smart-ass?"

"Oh! Oh! I know! Oh! Pick me!" Khani raised her hand in the air and thrashed it about.

"You kill me." His mouth quirked like it did most of the time he spent around her.

"Likewise, Street."

"Call me King."

Her nose wrinkled. "Not on your life."

He anticipated that sort of response. No one called him King and that suited him fine. He never cared for the name, but it was in essence who he was. Not a ruler. For him the name meant the opposite. Street was a distinguished member of an elite group of warriors. King was nobody. Less than nobody. He was the tarnish on society's silver service. And somehow his stigma was more intimate than his esteem.

"Why not?"

"Call me Queen." As the words poured from her lips her hands flew into the air. "I didn't mean it like that."

Like she was his? Not hardly. "Like what?" he asked, feigning innocence.

"You know what I'm talking about. On all accounts." She placed her hand over her mouth, refusing to speak.

"So, where am I going again?"

She slammed herself back onto the seat. "Turn around when you can. We missed the turn."

He laughed so hard his abs cramped.

"Shut it, would you?"

"If you put something in my mouth and make me." He grinned and wiggled his brow.

"Not going to happen."

"Stranger things have." He wheeled around at a gas station and headed back the way they'd come. "Just get your mind off my goods this time and let me know when to turn."

"You're hopeless."

"Never."

"Take your next right."

"Which would have been a left, had you not been distracted by how much you want my body. In the interest of our safety, I think I should go ahead and let you have your way with me."

Street turned at the next road and spared Khani a long glance. She buried her pretty face in her hands and shook her head. To his eternal pleasure a smile balled her blushed cheeks. Her head popped up. "It's three blocks up on the left."

The city beat slowed here, turning from restaurants and retail businesses to insurance and lawyers' offices. He pulled around the block, continued on to the opposite side of the square they needed, and then parked at the curb. "This should do. All of the other businesses looked deserted, but we'll play it safe."

Khani unfolded her legs and scooted forward. Her hand braced on the dash. She looked at something on the floorboard, and then lifted her gaze to him. Her hair curtained around the cliff of her jaw. "You don't play anything safe, do you?"

The street light filtered in through the windshield. It amplified the halo of black defining her iris. Her pupils expanded, adding to her allure and the amount of blood rushing to his extremities.

"Not much." He lifted his hand to her face. When she didn't break his hand off at the wrist his fingers skimmed her cheek. Her hair gathered atop his hand. "I find safe is scared and scared isn't secure."

"Sometimes fear is the only thing that saves you."

"Don't fear me." Street pulled his hand back slowly, savoring the silk of her hair across his knuckles.

"I should fear you most."

"Why?"

"Because I don't." She shoved him back into his seat.

Khani arched into the back seat and wrestled with her bag. Street's gaze lit on the small strip of creamy white skin that peaked out from beneath her blouse. His fingers itched to trace the flat expanse, to push the edge higher, and chart her belly button. His grip doubled on the steering wheel.

"Motherfuuuuu." Her expletive turned into a growl. The zipper of the small bag she fished out of the larger one caught on something. She stretched farther into the backseat.

He should have offered to help, but a bubble of pink skin scarred the now visible flesh at the side of her hip to the fringe of her shirt. Street had plenty of scars, a bullet wound on the shoulder, another on his chest, lashings over his bottom. Still he hadn't expected Khani to have such gnarly scars. Even in her line of work. Curiosity snacked on his frontal lobe.

She retrieved a small bag of tools from the back, and then slipped from the car, not sparing him a look. Maybe that was part of the reason she hadn't gotten naked with him. Before. But why wouldn't she let him put his hands on her?

The hatch opened. "Come on. They'll be open by the time you get a move on."

Street shook himself into the present, got out, and walked to the back of the SUV. "What's the plan?"

"Get in. Don't get caught." Her hand disappeared into a pocket. She pulled out a small digital decoder, and then stuffed it into her pocket. "Find Zeke's itinerary." With the push of a button the back hatch lowered. "Get out. Don't get caught." She turned away and tucked the pouch into the front of her trousers.

"I can handle that." He offered her his hand. She looked at it as though it were a magic trick she needed to master. "It doesn't have teeth."

"Ha." Her dark brow arched high.

"We're just a couple of co-workers doing some after-hours canoodling."

"You wish." She snatched his hand so hard she almost took it off.

He held it and spun her around. Amazingly, she went with the motion, twirling easily on the wet concrete. Their gazes locked. Street's heartbeat slowed as it always did before battle—winning Khani's affection would be the biggest of his life.

A second before he stepped forward, she shook off the trance. "Let's go. We don't have time for this." She tugged him down the sidewalk, keeping a full step ahead of him until they turned up the block.

"If you like my arm that much, you can chop it off and take it with you."

Her strides slowed and they fell into step together. "It's on the fourth floor of the six-story up ahead. Do you want to go in the front or back door?"

"Do you really have to ask?" A pointy finger poked in between his ribs, sending something akin to an itch but much funnier skating across his middle. He danced from the tickle and barked a laugh that startled him.

"No way," she gasped. "You're ticklish?"

"I don't know."

"What do you mean you don't know?" She swiveled, facing him, and walking backward.

"I'm not the kind of guy people tickle."

"Of course you're not, but what about when you were a kid?"

She'd just asked him about his past. He'd wanted her to just a few minutes ago. His tongue thickened. He could go all in or hash it up.

"Sorry." Khani whirled around. "I didn't mean to...never mind."

"You're the first person who's ever tickled me."

Her hand slipped through his fingers. Street let her go for now, feeling more raw than he ever expected. He wanted her to open up, but he never realized how much that asked, because he'd never disclosed things about himself people didn't already know from circumstance.

Khani waltzed past the alley with her head high and aimed for the glass-front double doors. Hand on the pull she stopped and pivoted toward him. "Unfasten my top two buttons, but don't make it obvious."

He sure as hell hadn't expected her to say that, but he'd be a Nancy not to seize the opportunity. Street lowered his mouth and sealed his lips over hers. Her gasp rolled across his tongue, eliciting a groan from the depths of his throat. His knuckles thrummed across her belly. He hit every button on his way to the top.

One finger slid beneath the thin fabric. His other hand followed the trail, ending on the cool front of the first clasped button. While his fingers worked the metal through the hole, Street worked his tongue across the edge of her mouth. Hers opened in invitation.

He held back. If he delved into the sweetness of her mouth, he'd lose all control and bonk her on the side of the building. His teeth raked her bottom lip, tugging it into his mouth. The chalky texture of her lipstick shielded her skin from the teasing strokes of his tongue. He longed to strip her mouth of the barrier just like he yearned to dismantle her other defenses. Street sucked her lip to a point, and then released it with a pop.

Seconds suspended between them. Piled atop one another. Khani blinked. "What the hell was that?"

"I made it obvious I was kissing you, not that I was unbuttoning your shirt. If you ask me though, the two go hand in hand."

Her shoulder-length hair thrashed side to side. "I was going to put the moves on the security guard to get upstairs. You were supposed to be my brother."

"You can't ask me to partially strip you without suffering the consequences. Why didn't you unfasten your own buttons?"

"The guard was looking at me. I didn't want to be conspicuous."

"Well, I definitely ruined your plan. But don't worry, I have another. Just hang back."

Chapter Eight

"He just about threw us into the elevator." In case there were any cameras, Khani blocked the knob with her body. The place wasn't high tech enough to need the decoder. She wiggled the J hook in the lock and glared at Street. "Did you threaten to castrate him?"

"Nah." Street shook his head in that slow, sexy way that had her heart free falling into her stomach. Calculating amusement twinkled in his hazel eyes.

"Well, what did you say?"

The lock gave. Khani pushed through the door, grabbed Street's arm and yanked him in behind her before she thought about the ramifications—just like she'd bloody done downstairs. He stepped so close static cracked between them. Literally, the material of her blouse clung to her torso. The wool blend of his pants charged the air—along with his smokin' physique.

Though close enough to meld their lips again, he didn't make the move. His gaze flitted about her face, searching for what, she hadn't a clue. But what she found in his eyes made his body seem paltry by comparison.

The more time she spent around him the harder it became to maintain her distance. The

issues that prohibited her from being with anyone—
even wanting to be with anyone—faded to the
background. Her carnal desire rushed forward.

Desire doesn't change the facts.

"I told him you had a thing for roof sex, that
you went wild for it. I said if he let us up no
questions, he could watch."

She'd never been amused by anyone she'd
had sex with, but this man beguiled her...and
damned if she knew what that meant.

Most of the time she never saw them after the
interaction. Only the club submissives, the guys
who frequented her haunt of choice, were safe to
cross her path, but they could never ask for a
repeat. Those were her rules. Rules she lived by.
Rules she'd do well to remember.

"Too bad for him and you, roof sex isn't my
thing." Khani freed him from her hold, skirted him,
and closed the door. The room sank into darkness
save for the twinkle of city lights coming through
the row of windows in the back of the office.

"Ever tried it?" His hot breath penetrated her
hair and accumulated at the back of her ear.

She'd let him at her back. How had that
happened? That never happened. Not without
major ramifications. She held perfectly still,
steeping in the remarkable peace that settled over
her. "No."

"You on top of everyone, taking your
pleasure. Dominating your lover. No holding back.
Screaming your orgasm for the world to hear. I
think you'd enjoy it."

"I think you'd enjoy it," she whispered. "You
should find a nice girl, another roof, and try it out."

"No."

Khani turned and pushed past him, barely
dodging a wastebasket in her haste. She wouldn't

ask why. It didn't matter. Finding her brother mattered.

Two desks occupied the small space. A dry erase board with a re-usable calendar hung on the exterior wall opposite the windows. Filing cabinets lined the interior wall. She moved to the first and opened the top drawer. "I made the reservations under my name. Check that board. If you don't find anything boot up the computer. Can you crack a firewall?"

"I can do lots of things," he said, ghosting through the space.

She turned back to the cabinet. Files hung back to back and filled the drawer close to overflowing. Numbers polluted the tabs, not names. Her hands flew over the markers. They ended fruitlessly at the back of the drawer. "Blast. They're coded, instead of organized by name."

"Are they dates?" He already sat behind the far desk, his fingers flying over the keys.

"Well, no. That would be too easy, wouldn't it?"

"You know, I like doing things the hard way too."

"Really?" she scoffed. "I hadn't noticed."

The drawer closed with a thwack.

"Weren't your directives don't get caught and, uh, don't get caught?"

"The guard is on the roof waiting for his show. Who's going to hear?"

"I'm just saying." He held one hand out in an, 'Okay, I told you so,' kind of way.

Khani turned to the desk nearest her and plopped into its high-backed chair. She depressed the power button, and waited.

"What? Are you racing me now?" Street jeered.

"Maybe. You scared?"

"Not a triffle. I'm already in."

"No way." The rollers on the chair worked like a gem. She pushed off the floor and zipped across the vinyl.

He prattled off the information lighting the screen. "Khani and Zeke Slaughter. March 2nd thru 8th, rescheduled. May 11th thru 18th, discount. Hotel Seward reserved for arrival and departure days. Days 1-2, Kenai National Wildlife Refuge. Day 3, Kenai Fjords National Park. Days 4-6, Denali National Park. Day 7, Denali National Park. Guide, Izzy. Paid in full."

"Will you..."

Before she could ask, Street pulled up another window and Googled Hotel Seward. While the Internet worked its magic, he opened the tour company's payroll program and scrolled through the list of twenty some-odd employees.

"Isay Polzin, 23, 225 Second Avenue, Seward, AK." He clicked to the search results, and then to a map. In fractions of a second he had their current location as well as the hotel's and guide's address in a neat list of directions. "Seward is two hundred kilometers away. And the two are five blocks apart. Do you want to hit the hotel or the guide's first?"

****

Khani meandered about the lobby, perusing pamphlets and the various long-dead animals stuffed and mounted for morbid viewing pleasure.

"Can I help you, miss?"

She turned to find the curvaceous mid-thirties woman she'd surveilled through the front glass step from the back office. "No thank you. I'm just waiting for my brother. You know how men are, always taking their sweet time."

"Ooh, where are you from? I adore your accent. It's so proper."

"I'm on holiday from London." Khani turned back to a multi-page brochure issued by the Wildlife Commission about bear safety for two reasons. One, she didn't want to engage this woman in conversation. That was Street's job. Two, half-ton carnivores with teeth and claws that ran up to 56 kilometers per hour made her palms sweat.

"Oh, how nice. If you need any tour recommendations, just let me know."

"Thanks."

They devoted the entire first two pages explaining how to save the *bear* from becoming mortality statistics since they were such a vital part of the ecosystem. She flipped to the middle. Rule one, don't feed the bears. *No worries.* Rule two, don't leave food, trash, pets, or small children unattended. *Did Street count as a child? Not a small one. So, they were okay* there. Rule three, if you encounter a bear, stay calm, break eye contact, and stand your ground. If the bear attacks, lie still on your belly, protecting your head and neck with your arms. Act passive. *Not bloody likely.* If the bear continues to maul you, then fight back using any available weapons: knife, rock, fist.

The door chimed and every nerve in Khani's highly trained body jumped like she was no more than a twit.

Fucking bears.

Street waltzed through the door and the woman's jaw hit the counter top. "Good evening." He smiled.

"H... Hi." The registrar visibly shook herself. "You must be the brother. My name is Tildy."

"A pleasure, Tildy." Street winked.

"I was just telling your sister, if you need any tour recommendations on your stay, I'd be happy to help." Tildy's lips curved into a sweet smile.

"I'd love to hear all about it after you tell me there's a room left in the inn with my name on it."

"Two rooms. I don't want to listen to you snore," Khani interjected.

"Two rooms then," Tildy nodded. "Since it's early in the season I have two side-by-side interior rooms, those are less expensive with no view, but have a cozy fireplace. I also have two side-by-side exterior rooms with a view of Resurrection Bay."

As the woman continued her spiel Khani roamed past the counter and Tildy's field of vision. She dipped under the breakaway counter, and then slipped through the open office door.

A massive desktop consumed most of the cluttered desk. Lights kaleidoscoped across the computer screen. Khani cleared the two steps in a whisper.

One bump of the mouse revealed a sea of open windows. She clicked through the options. Tildy had a legion of potential suitors distributed across six dating sites on the first heap of tabs. The last revealed the hotel's database. One click brought her to reservations. She chose the check-in, check-out log, and then scrolled to the last week.

Zeke Slaughter. Room 14, reserved May 10 and May 18. Second room canceled. Check-in, May 10. Check-out, May 11. No show, no cancelation for May 18.

Khani stood over the keyboard, stunned. When Zeke didn't call she'd known something was wrong. Having her suspicions confirmed iced her veins. Zeke had been her purpose for so long. She didn't need him near to function, but she needed him in the world. Without him the earth didn't rotate. Without him everything faded to black. Without him she wouldn't survive.

Street cleared his throat. The harsh noise jarred her out of the tailspin. With a few clicks she ordered the woman's screen and rushed to the door. She slowed at the threshold and listened.

"I need your signature right here and here," Tildy said.

She stole the opportunity, rounded the counter without incident, and leaned against the glass door, letting the chill exacerbate her misery.

"Ace." He leaned across the end of Hotel Seward's long counter. His shoulders bulged the fabric of his shirt. The older woman's eyes locked onto his sculpted beauty. Her cheeks flushed bright red. His hand extended toward the pen sticking up from the registrar's springy blonde bun. "Do you mind?" His voice took on a husk that could make any woman's knees buckle.

"No," she murmured.

Khani smiled at the exchange, her earlier jealousy over Street gone. Was it progress? She wished. It would simplify one problem.

"Cracking, Tildy. Thanks for your help." Street handed over the woman's pen and turned toward Khani. His gaze locked on her. The smile that had arched his mouth morphed into a hard line.

"Any time." The registrar waved after Street.

He practically shoved Khani out the front door and into the cold. "What is it? You look like the end of days is upon us."

"He stayed here the 10th, but didn't come back or cancel his reservation on the 18th."

"Looks like Mr. Polzin is due for some company." Street opened the passenger door to the SUV. "In you go."

"It's only a few blocks."

"And it's only a few degrees from freezing my nuts off. We don't want to risk that, now do we?"

"I've heard castrated men are more docile." She stepped onto the running boards, and then tucked into the vehicle. "Besides, it's not freezing yet."

"*You* want to make me docile, not have some wicked twist of fate do it." His sexual undertone wasn't lost on her. Nor was his beautiful mouth, strong and red from the cold.

He closed the door and hurried to his side. "You should probably go after Polzin. He's a young guy. Unless he's batting for the other team, you're our best bet at getting information out of him." Street pulled away from the curb and headed for the guide's address. "And it has to be freezing. There's bloody ice everywhere."

"What if he is?"

"Is what?"

"Batting for the other team?"

"Then I'll turn on the charm." He constricted his pecks, wobbling them at her.

"It's nice to see a man comfortable enough with his sexuality that a gay man hitting on him isn't cause for a full scale attack."

"Straight. Gay. A compliment is a compliment." He popped his collar. "I haven't heard you praise my new duds."

"And you won't."

"You know," he said, exacerbated, "they won't let you wear jeans, a tee, and trabs to the office with the LTC title. What a bag of garbage."

"What the hell are trabs?"

"Shoes. Tennies. Sport shoes."

Though she'd made a concerted effort not to engage Street in talk about anything personal, she had to know what was with his accent. "I thought you were from London."

"I am, but I spent some years—the formative ones, I guess—in Liverpool."

"The accent comes and goes," she conceded.

"I try to stow it completely, but old habits gob you."

She didn't know exactly what that meant, but agreed all the same.

Street wheeled them into a stubby driveway with a cabin at the end that looked like it had been tossed together by a drunk man. The south and west walls came together at an angle several degrees fewer than ninety. A naked bulb shined its dingy light on the two steps leading to the door. Five cars—prime candidates for junkyard scraps with their chipped paint and dents—crowded the front lawn.

Khani hadn't eaten in hours, but her stomach churned as though she'd just binged on a triple bacon cheeseburger and chili fries. She'd never pussed out on an assignment before. Damned if she was about to start. Family or not, her personal shit had to take a backseat. Or she could gob up the one mission that mattered the most.

She steeled her jittery nerves and exited the car. The mud immediately sucked at her feet, swelling around the edges of her black pointy toes. "All to pot." She kicked the excess goop and stamped off the rest. Shoulders back, gaze down, she avoided the biggest of the mess. Her steady strides gave no hint of the turmoil receding to the background. Thick drapes covered every window along the front of the house. As she walked her eyes tracked back and forth, covering her own six... even though Street had her ass covered at the very least.

A clubby electronic beat shook the asymmetrical walls. She took the stairs in one step and beat her fist against the door. Heavy voices cackled. One guys said, "The stripper is here." Their whoops and hollers grew two fold. She discerned at least seven different voices in the mix.

Every bit of unease vanished. Khani's body prepared for a confrontation. Her muscles loosened. Her breathing evened. Her senses honed to a needle's point. A needle didn't seem very vicious. Often the best offense was the one no one saw coming. The innocence of a needle vanished when you shoved it into someone's eyeball.

"Brava!" A young guy with brown floppy hair and a short beard opened the door wide.

Inside, seven men between the ages of eighteen and twenty or so held beer bottles in various stages of consumption. The oldest of them, presumably Isay Polzin, held a bottle of whisky in the crook of his thumb in the opposite hand that rested on the doorknob. He pinched a joint between his thumb and forefinger around the glass's red-waxed neck. The stench of it curled into the murky air of the cabin.

"Come in, pretty. Take off your clothes and we'll reward you sweetly." Isay hollered and slurred his words like a street beggar.

"Izzy?" she cooed.

"Yeah. Who's asking?" Isay's gaze hung on her still open buttons.

She felt a little bad for the guy. There wasn't much to see. "My name is Khani."

"Zdravstvuyte, Khani." He swept his arm encompassing the posse. "We're having a celebration. Come in and join us. We're really nice guys."

Khani jammed her hands into the back pocket of her slacks, pressed her meager breasts against the material of her shirt, and twisted in place. "I'd like to talk to you in private."

"Hear that, she wants my privates," he announced to the room. All the daft pricks laughed. One exceptional fool cupped his pitiful excuse for a dick and shook it at her. Their gazes flew from the lewd act to her, expecting a reaction of some sort.

Playing the hard-up cougar—not too far off if she considered Street—Khani's gaze dropped the Isay's crotch. A smile tickled her lips, but not for the reason he thought. If he knew what she'd planned for his goods, or if he didn't cooperate, he'd weep. "So, are you coming?"

"Oh, I'm coming." A moose-sized boy's hips thrust in an obscene display of alcohol and testosterone induced foolishness.

"We want to come too," the youngest—by looks anyway—shouted.

Two of the young men stood and started toward the door. Her patience vanished as did her playful demeanor. "Isay, this is your last chance to step outside and have a civil conversation with me."

"I don't even know you," the guide—to what, being an asshole?—contested.

The room collectively balked. "What are you, his mom?" the largest of the group derided.

"No. I'm not yours either, but I'll teach you a lesson," she purred.

Macho-man spread his arms in the doorway, nearly hitting Isay in the head with his fat hand. "Oh, I'd love to see you try."

Take out the leader and the rest will fall in line.

Khani struck so quickly no one gasped until she had Macho's limp cock and balls in her fist and twisted to face the back of the room. The big guy screamed like he'd yet to reach puberty. It only took another second for shock to subside. He scrambled back. Well, he tried.

The room erupted. The more horrified chaps clambered away, while his best friends surged forward. Too bad for Macho he only had two good friends in the bunch.

"Come any closer and I'll rip them off," she said in an even tone.

Macho's eyes bugged. With an impressive surge of adrenaline, he stopped trying to escape and lunged forward. His hands wrapped around Khani's neck. She dragged in a breath. When he squeezed she tensed the muscles in her neck and held it. Khani winked at the dummy and amplified her hold in proportion to his grasp on her throat.

"First time with your nuts in a vise," she squeaked. "Don't worry. With practice comes expertise. I've been in more choke holds than I can count." She relaxed the muscles in her neck, and then sucked a quick breath. Before his hands clamped on her wiggle room she stiffened her neck. "I can do this all day. Can you?"

His face reddened, while Isay's paled. A tear seeped from Macho's big brown eyes and slipped down his cheek. His hands fell away from her neck. "Please," he whimpered.

She shook her head. "Only if your friend agrees to speak to me outside."

"Izzy, fuck! Come on, man." Macho's bloodshot gaze sliced to his friend.

"Just let him the hell go." Isay put both hands in the air, his bottle and joint now dangling in each.

"Remember this the next time you're in the presence of a young woman, and show some respect. You never know what she's capable of."

"She's capable of getting her ass beat," one of the young sheep in the back hollered.

"If you're the man to do it, please step forward." Khani stood her ground, ignoring the throbbing of her head. No matter how many times it happened, it never got painless. When none of them made their play she turned to Isay and hiked her thumb toward the lawn. She eyed the group. "If any or all of you get the big idea to step outside and prove yourself a man, I'll make sure Izzy never reproduces."

She closed the door behind her and shoved the kid in the direction of the largest truck in the lawn. "Just in case your friends get any big ideas, we'll talk behind the truck."

The kid raised the bottle to his lips. Khani snatched it away and poured the remaining liquid onto the dirt. "What the...what do you want, lady?"

"Who is your employer?"

"Alaska Adventure, why?"

"How was your last excursion?"

"Great. I got head while the girl's parents slept in the next tent."

Khani ignored the crudeness. "When was that?"

"I don't keep a calendar of all my sexual interaction." His mouth screwed into a cocky sneer.

"Surly you remember the dates of your last guide excursion." She sharpened her gaze, and then let it drop to the front of his pants.

"Khorosho. Khorosho," he said, flailing his arms.

"I'm English, not Russian, you rat-arsed piece."

"All right. All right," he shook his hands again. "I guided the first week of this month."

"What about last week?"

"Ah." The kid shooed it off. "It got canceled."

Khani stepped forward. "By whom?"

"Chill." Isay treaded backward. "The big guy, the one I was supposed to guide, canceled."

"What was his name?"

"Hell, I don't know. Why does it matter?" He widened his hands toward the sky.

"Because you want to have full function of your penis, Isay. That's why."

"His name..." The kid pushed the heel of his hand to the bridge of his nose. "His name was Killer...something...I can't remember. I'm really lit right now." His swollen pupils begged off.

"You're about to be lit in a whole new way, bloke." Khani dropped her hand from her hip.

He jumped back. "Jesus, his name was zzz... Zeke...Zeke Slaughter. He wanted to go by himself. He paid me in full, and then took off on his own."

"Why hold out on me, Isay?"

His head shook side to side. "I could lose my job for letting him go alone." He dropped on the joint, and then placed his palms together. "You can't say anything. Please."

"Where did he go?"

"I don't know."

"When he told you he wanted to cancel where were you?"

"At the campground at Copper Landing near Kenai Lake and the Russian River."

"Where would he have gone?"

"There are over a million acres in the Kenai Refuge. Fuck if I know." Isay rubbed his forehead. "Are we done yet?"

"What about the others in the group?"

"The family of five due to tour canceled. Half the family started puking the day before they were going to fly out of wherever the hell they were coming from." The kid flicked his wrist as though a family of five matter no more than a speck of dirt.

"So, you let him wander into the middle of nowhere all by himself?"

"It's not like he was helpless. He looked like he could handle shit." His scrawny shoulders rolled in a near boneless sway.

He had a point. She'd trust Zeke to do a better job navigating the wilderness than she would this shit. "How the hell did you get to be responsible for people's lives?"

"I grew up roaming these parks."

"And?"

"My uncle owns the company."

And there was her answer. She sneered. "Get out of my face, Isay."

"Yeah, all right." He teetered across the small dirt lawn, his feet leaving deep prints in the mud.

Khani looked down at her ruined shoes. The disappointment that had nothing to do with boots weighted her more than the extra muck. She stamped the few feet to the SUV and flung herself inside without looking at Street.

"What were they celebrating?" he asked.

"Being asshats. Please, just drive."

The vehicle eased out of the drive and headed up the road. Relief, the tiniest bit of it, eased one of the cramps in her brain. She sank back into the seat and tried to think about what she knew, but a piercing headache blanketed all thought. Her eyes closed out the blurring lights. Two minutes later the car stopped. She blinked in the neon open sign on the low-key tavern.

"You need to eat. I need to eat." Street shut off the engine and climbed out of the car.

She could sit here for the forty or more minutes it took him to eat or she could go inside and hope her appetite returned. Her door opened and Street stood there waiting with a reticence she truly appreciated. Her mud-caked boots slopped across the plastic floor mat, and then plopped onto the concrete sidewalk. He closed the car door and walked ahead, grabbing the handle of the pub's door and opening it for her.

"What are you, some kind of gentleman?"

"Not a chance."

On safe-mode so she didn't totally flip her shit, Khani followed demurely behind Street to a four-seater booth. She slid in across from him and stared into his eyes, which reflected the green neon of a beer brand she'd never seen before.

"What'll you have?" the burliest server in all the world grumbled.

"Two waters, two pints of the best dark you have, and a menu, thanks," Street said.

The man grunted his compliance as he shoved off.

Street knocked the table with his knuckles, slowly at first and then faster and faster.

"Say what you have to say already," she snapped.

"He was lying?"

"The waiter didn't say anything." She flashed an imitation grin.

"That's not who I'm talking about and you know it." He rested his elbows on the table.

She flattened her hands on the table. "You were in the car. You don't even know what Isay said. So, how the hell do you know he was lying?"

"I read his body language."

"Oh, you're a good interpreter of drunken stumbles and higher than the sky gestures?"

"Reading people is what I do. That's why I moved up so fast in the Branch office." He dragged in a breath and his brow furrowed. "I've had specific training that allows me to tell with upward of ninety-percent accuracy whether or not people are telling the truth."

"Even when you're stuck in a vehicle and not talking to them?"

He folded his big arms over his chest. "It's easier when I've talked to them for a while, identified a base-line, and questioned them for longer. But I'm telling you now, he was lying."

"Isay didn't want to tell me Zeke paid him to let him go into the fucking underworld by himself. If his uncle, a-k-a his employer, knew, he'd get fired."

"And you believe that?" Street arched a brow.

"If something happens to their patron while on their roster, they could be held liable, especially if there was negligence on the part of the company."

He lowered his head. "I want to talk to him."

"There's nothing he can do for us...me. He doesn't know where Zeke is."

The server smacked down their foam-topped beers in tandem, stalked to the bar, and then headed back with two pints of water. He delivered them in the same brutish method. Khani nodded at him, liking his style. No nonsense.

Street took a long pull of creamy foam. "What did he know?"

"He last saw Zeke on the west side of the park, at the Copper Landing campground, close to where Kenai Lake and the Russian River meet. Oh." She lifted a finger. "And that the Kenai Park is a million bloody acres around." Khani chugged the first third of her frothy pint.

"How's your neck?" That green tinted gaze caressed her tender throat.

"Fine." She took another swig. "He was a pussy."

"The clamp he had on you didn't look too slight from my vantage point."

"You didn't see the clamp I had on him." She pointed her finger at his chest.

His face contorted. "I saw enough to know he won't walk right for a week."

"He earned it."

"Without a doubt. But it still hurts me." He shifted in the seat and adjusted his trousers.

"Thank you," she whispered.

"For what, letting you get choked?"

"Yes," she nodded.

"You're nuts." He laughed.

"Thank you for not charging into the middle of it. Thank you for letting me handle the situation."

"If I'd thought you'd needed help, I'd have busted all their heads no matter how mad you got." He leaned back against the seat. "Those kids were punks. You could have taken them all on at once." He drummed the table with his thumbs. "I was actually kind of hoping they'd make a go at you."

"I bet you were."

"I was bored."

"After we eat, we can head out to Kenai and —"

Street shook his head. "We'll pack up tonight, get a few hours of sleep, and be at the campground by dawn. We won't do anyone good by getting lost in the middle of blasted nowhere."

"Look who's bossy now."

Chapter Nine

What had the kid been lying about?

Street dragged the razor over his cheek. The quad-blades blazed a trail through the suds, leaving smooth skin in its wake. He maneuvered the cutting edge around his ear lobe, and then rinsed the tool under the steaming water.

Isay Polzin lived by his own set of rules. The blatant use of alcohol and illegal drugs said as much. If he wasn't worried about getting hauled to jail over some pot, what did he have to hide?

He cupped water into his palms and washed away the excess soap. The warm water soothed the tiny nick he'd carved out of his neck. Water pooled in his hands and he submerged his face in it as much as he could and held his breath, willing his desire away. He wanted answers. He wanted Khani more.

Three hand-jobs in as many hours had only provoked his body and deteriorated his self-control. His gaze slid to the glowing red clock on the end table sandwiched between two queen beds. He'd only slept on one. *What a waste.*

Twilight started at the unholy hour of three forty a.m. with sunrise following an hour behind. The digital readout said he had just enough time to rub one out, get dressed, and then meet Khani in the lobby. Street cupped his sore balls and massaged away the ache, which would only multiply with another orgasm so closely behind the last three. They relaxed into his touch. He lifted his chin, closed his eyes, and pictured her long legs wrapped around his waist.

A groan echoed off the bathroom walls. His touch moved higher, toying with his sensitive skin before he palmed the solid length. Stroke by stroke his hips joined the lightly rising tempo of motion.

Three abrupt knocks ricocheted through the room and his thickening haze of lust.

"Fuck me hard, why don't you?"

A small, but insistent hand wrapped on the door again.

Street released his reddened cock with another soft curse and stalked through the room. Through the peephole he watched Khani lift her fist to knock again. He snatched the door open before she made contact. "You're early," he barked.

Her gaze widened for a second, and then tightened on his erect dick. The grey of her eyes clouded. She squeezed the rucksack's strap so hard the padded fabric crinkled under grip.

His cock bobbed in appreciation of her reaction. His lungs tightened. He waited for her to do something. To say something. 'Get on the bed,' ranked high on his list of things he silently begged her to say.

Khani's lips parted. Her breaths came in shallow pants. "Sorry for the interruption."

She extended her index finger, and then swiped it across the slit at the crown of his cock. The touch lit his fuse, burning it to the very edge of his skin. Khani studied the clear pre-cum beaded on the end of her finger. Her pink tongue extended.

She swiped the evidence of his desire off the tip of her finger. His heart exploded inside his chest.

Her tongue rolled around her mouth. Her eyes closed. A moan purred in the back of her throat.

Like a loyal dog, he stood rock solid and eager to follow her instructions. Ten years ago the notion that he'd follow anyone's instructions— especially a woman's half his size—would've stitched his sides in laughter. But there was nothing funny about Khani's blatant passion and the need she had for control. Even more sobering was his willingness to give her what she needed.

Slowly her lids fluttered opened. She licked her lips, and then her mouth formed a solid line. "Get dressed. We have shit to do."

The words punched him in the nuts. He wrestled with the pain of rejection and the arguments poised on the end of his tongue. She obviously wanted him. He was blatantly willing. His ornery cock refused to submit.

Street scrubbed a hand over his face. He moved to the bed, snatched his boxers, and then shoved his legs inside. Grey hiking pants to his white tee, she stood in the open doorway and watched him dress. Instead of deflating, he grew impossibly harder. How did she make getting dressed a form of foreplay? He dove into his light jacket and jerked his pack onto his shoulder.

"Ready, mum."

"I'm driving."

He almost said, 'no shit,' but he clenched his jaw and followed her out the door and into the stairwell. Her almost black hair bounced as she descended the flight with rapid stamps of her treaded boots. Out the front door the SUV idled by the curb. Its lights cut through the darkness.

"When did you wake up?"

She hurried ahead. "Couldn't go to sleep."

"You should've come by earlier. I know a good way to beat insomnia."

"That wouldn't have helped me sleep." She tossed her gear into the back and hurried to the driver's seat.

Oh, he could fuck her into unconsciousness, if she'd let him. But what little trust he'd gained with her seemed to be slipping through his fingers. Street deposited his sack beside her lopsided one. They left the long-range rifles and heavy artillery behind, since this was a scouting mission of sorts. As it was, the two bags nearly devoured the entire footprint of the back. He righted hers, closed the hatch, and climbed into the passenger seat.

"How long has it been since you've slept?" he asked.

Khani shifted the vehicle to drive. "About forty-eight hours now."

"If you don't take care of yourself, you won't do Zeke any good."

"Like forty-eight is a big deal. You know it's not." She rocketed away from the hotel.

"Buckle up." Street gave the order and pulled his own safety belt into place.

"Fuck you."

"Even better."

A breath snorted through her nostrils. She took the corner so hard Street grabbed the oh-shit handle near his head.

"You can buckle it or I will," he said.

"I'd love to see you try," she challenged.

"I bet you would." He dropped his grip. The handle smacked the SUV's roof. He shifted and the leather beneath him squeaked.

She yanked the buckle across her chest and stabbed it into the receiver. The click rang off the windows.

"And forty-eight isn't bad when you're in the middle of a mission, but I have a suspicion we've just started this adventure."

"If you don't close your mouth, I'm going to use my ball-gag on you."

"You have one of those?"

She snapped her gaze to his and rolled her eyes before returning her attention to the road. "What do you think?"

"I think you need control to be able to get off, but I didn't think you were a full-on dominatrix."

"Maybe you're not as smart as you think you are." A hostile grin contorted her red lips.

This woman had rolled until midnight and had been ready to go again at three a.m. with no sleep to speak of over the last two days and still make-up perfectly accentuated her face. Why? Who the hell did she have to impress in a town where flannel and feather-stuffed jackets were all the rage? It certainly wasn't him. She only used him to hone her latest torture techniques.

Khani drove like the sunrise would turn them to a pile of ashes. Her gaze bounded from the road, to the clock lighting the dash, to the left where the burning ball of gas brightened the sky one lumen at a time.

"Stop worrying."

"Stop talking," she snapped.

"Hikers won't set out until sunrise and most of the people near the lakes and rivers are there to fish. They'll hang around shore at the campground all day."

"I'm really going to have to teach you how to listen."

"Promises. Promises."

Her head shook back and forth. "You're not a submissive."

"No, but I could be yours."

She straightened and rolled her shoulders. "It doesn't work that way. You either crave it or you don't."

"Khani..." He waited until her gaze met his. It took two-and-a-half miles for her relent. Only when their gazes locked in a dangerous embrace did he speak. "I crave you."

The car slowed. Their gazes held for too long on the winding valley roads. His heart beat double-time. Her head jerked back to the windshield with a huff.

Grey cotton-candy clouds stuck to the tops of the mountains on either side of the vehicle. They thickened the air and revealed the source of all slicked streets and saturated ground. On their left a swollen river weaved through the valley, bowing and arching at the roadside. To the right sheered off slopes stood as impassable sentries to the wilderness.

"We're getting close to the campground. Take my phone and send the latest picture in my camera roll to your phone. It's the last picture I have of Zeke."

"It won't be the last," he said, praying he was right.

"We'll split up the immediate area. Use the picture. Look for him. Ask people if they've seen him."

He didn't bother telling her he knew how to search for someone.

"Also, watch your ass. If he knows a giant is looking for him and doesn't know I'm there, he might come after you."

"Awe, you're worried about me. How cute," he cooed.

"You think Seward has a kink store?" She slid a smirk over her shoulder. "I don't think I can wait 'till DC for that gag."

Street chuckled and grabbed her phone. He transferred the picture, and then stared at it for a minute. He'd done research on Zeke, as much as he'd dared without pissing her off. He'd seen a picture of the man before. The chap had been decked in black with bronze stars, his chin stony, eyes sharp, and shoulders at attention in his Royal Marines dress uniform. In the picture on the screen he looked like a different man. He donned nice leather shoes, jeans, and a casual sweater. His cheeks stretched wide in a grin and his eyes rolled slightly up as though he'd only allowed the picture to appease his sister.

"How do all these people have time to be fishing in the middle of the day? Don't they have jobs?" she asked.

When he lifted his gaze more than thirty cars filled the blacktopped lot and another handful crowded the dark gravel extension. Past it, RV's and tents sprinkled across the green grass. Half the occupants already dressed in hip-waders lined the shore almost shoulder to shoulder in what Street guessed were the best spots. Only a few lines breached the water. Most anglers situated their gear, checked their lines, and watched the rushing water.

"Most of the jobs in Alaska are seasonal. And you're looking at one of them. Besides, a person could feed their family for a year with a good spring catch."

"If you're right, maybe we'll get lucky and some of them will have seen Zeke. He was here nine days ago."

"According to Isay."

"Yes, according to the guide who was supposed to lead him through the three parks over seven days."

"But didn't," he reminded. "That seems lavvy to me."

"Lavvy?"

"Like the toilet. Stinky. Suspicious."

"You don't know my brother."

"No, but I know people and business. If anything happened to your brother when they were supposed to be guiding him, that's their company gone."

"But Isay didn't tell them."

"It's a bloody small town and that boy isn't quiet about anything. You really think they didn't know he was in Seward gettin' bevvied every night?"

Khani opened her mouth, but no words came out. She clamped it shut. Her lips wiggled back and forth. "Aren't they worried about bears?"

Avoidance. He should have expected as much. It's what she did. "Only the slowest one," he chuckled.

"It's not funny," she snapped.

He laughed about, her evasion not the bears, but she didn't know that.

Khani whipped the SUV into an impossibly tight spot between a dually and a truck with wheels that would hit him mid-thigh. "Did you know one swipe of a grizzly's paw can kill a person?"

"Did you know one strike of your little fist can kill a person? And you're a quarter of the size of one of those things."

"That's why it…" She clamped her mouth closed and shook her head. "Forget it." Khani swooshed him away with her hand and climbed out of the car. Squeezed was the more accurate term.

Luckily she'd given him more room. He sucked in things that wouldn't move on an inhale and hobbled on tip-toes toward the back of the car. "I hope we don't have to make a fast getaway. You know, from a bear or something."

Her finger poked into his side with enough force that he winced. "It's not funny."

"That you—a trained operative, who has faced down mass murderers and mob lords—are scared of being attacked by a grizzly bear? Yeah, it's a little funny." He winked.

"There aren't any big predators in all of the United Kingdom," she growled.

"Not right now, because I'm here, with you."

"Just make sure your weapon is easily accessible and you have an extra magazine, and come on." Khani hiked her pack onto her shoulders and then tightened the straps.

Street locked down the urge to laugh. It truly tickled him that the toughest person he knew, one who'd never shown an ounce of weakness, strapped on the pack like it were a life preserver and she was diving into the middle of the ocean. And damn it, it endeared her to him even more. He groaned, grabbed his sack, and slung it onto his back. Under his hand the back hatch closed with a resounding *boom*.

She surveilled the area with a sweeping gaze. "I'll take the east side."

"Sure, *you* take the roadside with over half our target group and send me to the woods to be supper."

"You played rugby, right?" Her bronzed eyelids lifted.

"How'd you know? Been checking up on me, 'ey?"

"Look at you." She flourished her hand down his body. "You could take a juvenile bear."

"What about a ma bear or the da?"

Her small shoulders bobbed. "Then you shoot the guy next to you, run like hell, and hope there is only one of them or that you packed that extra clip I told you to." With that she pivoted and strode to her section of the grounds.

Being a guy who dwarfed most of the population, he'd learned the subtle approach intimidated the least. Street ambled toward the bank. He popped the collar on his jacket against the slicing wind and cursed. The only thing he hated worse than cold was hunger so voracious it used his spinal cord as dental floss. His heavily treaded boot threatened to lose traction on the slick lining the bulging river.

Millions of gallons of glacial melt whirled past him with little more than a murmured ripple. The sheer power of nature once more took his breath. It gave life and took it in the blink of an eye. He crouched at the burbling edge in between two fishermen and submerged the tips of his fingers. The current swept his hand the two feet he allowed it before tugging his hands from the run.

"Colder than my ex-wife before alimony."

Street craned his head to regard the bloke to his left. A red beard hung to the first buttons of his red and black flannel jacket. Cork covered a third of the well-used fishing rod he twitched back and forth with a narrow wrist.

"Is that so?" Street asked.

"Ha. I knew you wasn't from 'round here. And hell yeah it's so. She's settled since I started lining her pockets with better than half my catch. But man, she could yell the skin off a elk."

"So you fish here a lot?"

"Every damn day, now that she's bleedin' me. You lookin' for a good fishin' hole? Then this is it. Right now, at least. Later in the season you'll have to move farther downriver to get the good ones."

"I'm actually looking for a friend. He was last seen here a week ago Monday. You mind taking a look at this picture?" Street held out the phone before the man answered. "His name's Zeke. He's a couple of inches shorter than me."

The man squinted at the picture, and then angled his gaze at Street. "Well stand up, son. So I can see you."

He extended to his full height. The man's head followed him up. It lolled back and the man blinked. "Shit. You're what, six five?"

"My friend is six four, almost black hair, grey eyes," he countered.

"As wide as you?"

"Muscles, but sleeker."

Murky blue eyes zeroed in on the phone again. "Mind if I hold it?"

Street handed over the phone. After another moment, the bloke shook his head. "Na, I ain't seen him. Andrew!" He stepped around Street and thrust the phone at another fisherman. "You saw this guy, Monday week? Little smaller than this bull." His thumb hiked at Street.

Andrew looked for a minute. "No way you'd see a dude that big and not remember. And I's here sun-up to sun-down Monday thru Friday. Never saw him. Now, that don't mean he wasn't out here. Just means I didn't see him. But so you know, I like to keep tabs on my competition." He handed the phone over. "You plannin' to be my competition?"

"No, sir."

"Good," Andrew said, "I have about all I can take out here already." His line drew tight and pulled his attention with it.

"Lucky bastard," red beard growled. He thrust the phone back at Street, and then gave his line a tug.

"Well, thanks for your help," Street said.

"No trouble." The bloke yanked on his rod in rapid beats.

Street stepped away, but stopped himself. He shouldn't give a shit, but he did. Like it or not. "You have kids?"

"Three."

"Your ex have them?"

"Yep. My son, well, my oldest son'll graduate high school next year."

He stepped closer and lowered his gaze to the chap's. "Then quit bitching about your money-grubbing ex-wife and take responsibility for your kids. One day they'll be adults and you'll want to look them in the eye without feeling like you're a two-inch prick."

The man faltered as though Street had punched him. Anger replaced surprise. Street held his gaze, hoping the meaning settled. Slowly, the sneer melted into a thin line.

He bowed and headed up the shore toward the next group of fishermen. "Sorry to interrupt, but Andrew told me to ask you guys. I'm looking for my friend." Street went through the next three groups the same way. No one had seen Zeke.

Street stepped back from the river and found Khani plowing through her batch of fisherman as though she worked a line-up of suspects. The rate she filtered through her group told him she had no better luck.

The rock boundary of the excess parking lot turned to thick brown grass with spruce trees scattered about its gradual incline. A beaten-down mud path led into the distance. He wondered if it was a walking trail or a convenient pee spot for the fishermen. His gaze scanned the campground. In a smattering of navy-blue and green domed tents, two hikers climbed out of a tiny orange two-man made light for long trips into the wild.

They stretched their arms above their heads and arched out the restriction of such a cramped space. Each hobbled into their respective boots laid on a tarp in front of the zipper door. They slung on small bags, and then the woman leaned over and lifted a walking stick from the ground. She extended it toward the man. His upper lip curled. He eyed the thing as though it were barbed before finally relenting.

Slowly, they headed toward the trail's mouth, the walking sticks a third party between them. Street played a hunch and set out for the trailhead without Khani. The woman twirled the end of a long braid around her index finger. She exaggerated her lumbering side-to-side as though she were bored, while the bloke favored one knee and pushed to keep pace.

Street timed it so they all came to the soggy path at the same time. "Oh, I'm sorry." He shuffled back and put both hands up in surrender.

"No." The bloke leaned heavily of the stick and ushered Street ahead with a flourish. "Go ahead." The young woman's jaw worked, but she held her tongue.

"Really, you go. I'm waiting on my girlfriend," Street insisted. "I was just checking out the trail. Have you been here before? How is it?"

"It's okay—"

His woman cut him off. "Do you hike a lot? You look like an experienced hiker, but you're not from around here, are you?"

"I've done my fair share of outdoor living," Street smiled. "But here, we're tourists."

"No you're not. Tourists walk around in groups of ten. You're adventurers. This trail will bore you to tears. It's easy in, easier out." She looked to her man and grimaced. 'Sorry,' she mouthed. "He's recovering from MCL surgery. Otherwise we'd be on the ice-fields right now. Those are fun and challenging."

"So challenging I ripped my MCL," the bloke reminded.

"Well, ah, thanks for the advice," he inclined his head to the couple. "Good luck on your recovery."

They nodded and headed gingerly up the trail. Street turned and found Khani stomping in his direction. "What is it?"

"These people haven't seen dick." Her fists clenched at her sides. "It pisses me off, okay?" She shook them before folding her arms across her middle.

"Okay."

"Okay?" Her mouth arched wide as she dragged out the word. "You're just going to let me bite your head off for no good reason?"

"You're worried about your family." He scrubbed the back of his hand over his frosty nose. "I can't say I know what you're going through, but I understand where your angst comes from. So, yeah. I am."

Her cerulean eyes rolled back into her head. "Why do you have to be so logical? Fight with me, would you?"

"It wouldn't make you feel better, but I know something that would."

"You found a lead?"

"No, I was thinking more along the lines of eating you out."

She grunted and shoved at his chest.

"Kidding," he laughed.

Khani fought the curving of her lips.

"Your brother wasn't here at all. Most of the fishermen I talked to are here every day from dawn until dusk. They're protective of their fishing ground. An outsider would stand out like a black eye."

"He's sneaky. Maybe he blended in," she countered.

"What reason would he have to go incognito up here?"

"I don't know. None." Her little hands balled into lethal fists. "But there are trails all around here. Suppose he slipped up one without anyone seeing him."

"Is your brother a risk taker or play-it-safe kind of guy?"

"What do you think?"

"If he's anything like you, he'll risk his body all day long, but never his heart."

She reeled back. Her gaze diminished to slits. "I don't have a heart."

"Sure you do. It's just behind a few kilometers of concrete and steel mesh."

"Oh yeah, well where's yours?"

He pointed his index finger at her chest. "Standing in front of me, looking like she wants to rip me from limp to limb."

Khani's hands came up like a shield. The whites circling her eyes grew two fold. She turned and started to walk away...just like she always did.

"In a BDSM relationship, a master—"

Her feet ground into the rocks. "Dominant," she snapped. "Not master. I'm no one's master."

"Fine. In a dominant, submissive relationship, there's trust, right?"

"On both sides," she agreed.

"You may not be my Dominant, but I'm asking you to start trusting me. Everything I do is to help you. Help you find your brother. Help you find yourself."

"I know myself, thank you."

He took a step forward and spoke into her ear. "No you don't. No more than I know myself. We're getting closer, but we have a way to go." He rounded her, planting himself as a physical barrier yet again. "Isay lied. Your brother wouldn't waste his time fishing or hiking a toddler trail. Troop, I'll never hurt you. So, please trust me on this." He grabbed the keys from her hand and headed for the car. The seconds gathered with no movement behind him. A stitch tightened in his chest. He swallowed past his doubt and soldiered on.

Street reached for the SUV's handle.

Her slow and gentle treads grew near. "Troop?"

"Trooper," he explained.

"Now I have a pet name." She groaned. "Fine, we'll try it your way."

Chapter Ten

Isay's toes pointed better than a Royal Opera House prima ballerina's. His back arched in a near perfect C. Long, muscular legs scissored in search of the ground. He wouldn't make company though. The contorted muscles and high red flush of his face just weren't entertainment material. Not for the general public, at least.

Khani eased into the recliner and crossed her legs. "What an intriguing show," she cooed. "I don't know why I didn't let you do this sooner." Then again, maybe not. Her clit throbbed against the seam of her pants. The closeness of her black lace bra abraded her stiff nipples every time she moved. Watching Street work only incited her need to claim him. She'd licked his pre-cum to show him how unaffected she was by his presence. The moment his taste hit her tongue the impulse exploded in her face.

She wanted him now more than ever. So much so that for a moment she forgot the entire reason for their being here.

His harsh gaze remained locked on Isay's. "I don't know why either. I'm quite enjoying myself. Perhaps he'll hold out for a while yet. Five minutes is four and a half longer than I expected him to last."

The punk garbled through the sock shoved in his mouth.

"What was that? I need to up the ante?" Street pursed his lips as though thinking about his options. "Why, Isay, I believe you're right. I'm going to set you down again. If you don't tell me what I want to know, I'll use your cock and balls as my next handles." He untwisted the fists full of the bloke's nipples, gently lowered him to the floor, and then yanked the white fabric from his stuffed lips.

She remembered now.

A red handprint stained the kid's neck. His shirt hung half off his body, ripped down the front from when he'd tried to escape. Pale skin inflated and deflated at a stressful pace, emphasizing his skeletal frame.

"Talk. Now." Street cupped the air and squeezed. "Or I get a handful."

Isay screwed his lips tight.

"You think he has that much?" Khani asked.

"Only one way to find out." Street stepped forward.

"Wait. Fucking wait!" He covered his chest with one hand and his junk with the other. "I saw him, okay? But not at the campground."

Khani leapt to her feet without making the decision to do so. "Where? When?"

He stiffened. "I guided him to Exit Glacier Monday." When his mouth quit moving Street nudged him with a finger to the forehead. "We hiked hard all day into the ice-field. We made camp that night, and then..." The bastard hugged himself. As though those skinny arms could save him.

Khani lunged. She crouched and rammed her shoulder into the weak belly. Her knee split his knees. With one easy push she laid him flat on his back. She pressed her forearm on his windpipe and released her fury, fear, and frustration in a scream. "Where is my brother?"

Air wheezed through purple lips. She roared and pressed harder. The edge of reason blurred. Tightness clamped her waist and she dangled above the piece of shit on the ground.

"He won't do you any good dead." Street's chest met her back.

Strangely she sank into it completely spent and oddly at ease in his embrace. She panted much like Isay had, her breaths whooshing through her nose and open mouth.

The punk rolled to his side. He tucked into a gagging ball.

Street set her on the floor, but held firmly to her middle. "Talk, kid, or I'll let her go."

A hack that'd make a life-long smoker cringe erupted from his throat. "I left him," he rasped. "I left all my gear behind, so he wouldn't hear me leave. A set of back-up gear had been stowed a mile up an alternate trail. I hiked all night. Got back here about lunchtime the next day."

"Did you have a big date or just felt like fuckin' off?" Khani asked.

"I'd asked for the time off, but my uncle wouldn't give it to me." He swallowed and grimaced. His fingers tested the skin at his throat. "I just wanted to show him, you know?"

"I know you're a piece of shit with no regard for anyone but yourself," Khani spat.

The hand holding her back slid across her torso, releasing her. Street's wide frame stepped around her and advanced on Isay. His shoulders shifted with each step, prowling. Hefty thighs moved quietly over the creaky wooden floor. Isay scrambled back on elbows and heels, but Street didn't stop until he towered over the prone form. "I know you're lying. I can see it on your face. I also know you wouldn't trash two days, hiking all the way out there to stow a pack and then back, just to hack off your uncle." He leaned down, hands extended toward the bastard's pecker.

"No! Yes! I mean yes, I lied." Each word pitched higher than the last. "My uncle paid me double to ditch him at the pass."

Khani's heart stuttered.

Street's hand hovered over the guy's goods. "Why would he do that?"

"You'll have to ask him. I really don't fucking know. I swear!" Tears ran down Isay's cheek.

"The problem is," Street *tsk*ed, "once a liar, always a liar."

****

Khani paced from one window to the next along the front of the house, waiting for her computer to confirm the tap she'd placed on Uncle Vasaya's phone to come on line. She ignored the carcasses of burned down joints and bottle caps beneath her feet. Her mind prodded the more pressing problem at hand. Who was Isay Polzin's uncle and why would he order his nephew to abandon a client on the middle of a mother f'ing glacier during the melting season?

"Good job, Isay." Street patted him on the head. The reforming punk sat strapped with duct tape to the recliner Khani had used. His knees gaped. His fingers spread wide. His head remained free to see the horrors his limbs would endure, if he refused to make the call. Street crouched to eye level. "I think we've finally arrived at an understanding. You get your uncle here without him suspecting anything, you live. You alert him in any way, you die. And then we find your uncle anyway."

"He's my only family." The young man hung his head. Tears dripped off the end of his nose, spilling into the puddle at his lap. "He gave me this house, his old office, to live in after my parents kicked me out."

The progress bar zipped across the computer screen, and then flashed confirmation. "It's ready." Khani squatted in front of the keyboard and struck off a few lines of code. They allowed her to end the call at any moment.

"Remember that. You want him to live, you cooperate." Street pressed send on Isay's phone, activated the speakerphone, and then held it out for the kid. "Just like we practiced and tomorrow this will just be the worst hangover of your life."

"Isay, damnit, you cost me double last night," Vasaya answered without greeting. "The whole goddammned street called the station about your party. Winslow demanded double what I usually pay him to look the other way. It's your good fortune I had the extra den'gi to pay."

"I...I'm sorry, my boys got out of control." Isay gulped. "Look, I need to talk to you about something."

"You didn't get girl knocked up again, did you? Because I don't think you're lucky enough for two miscarriages."

Khani's stomach tucked and dove into her lower intestines. She wanted kids like she wanted a bullet to the head, but it didn't mean she didn't have a soft spot for the helpless things. Street's upper lip arched in a silent snarl.

"Naw. Naw. It's about that thing you had me do the—"

"Have I taught you nothing? Don't talk about shit over the phone. You want to talk about stuff, you come see me."

"I can't."

Her hand hovered over the disconnect key, while Street's trigger finger poised on the guard of his customized Smith & Wesson E-series.

"Excuse me? What do you mean you can't?"

"I've got the shits. I can't leave the toilet for more than a couple minutes."

"I swear to Christ, you're more trouble than you're worth sometimes." Vasaya huffed a protracted breath, crackling the line. "Can it wait?"

"Naw. I wouldn't 'a called you out to see me like this, if it could."

"I'll be there in five," the uncle said before disconnecting the call.

"Good choice, Isay. You know, life is the consequence of the choices people make. Choose wrong and the ripple effect is beyond the scope of your ability to reason."

No shit.

If Khani had known how deep that first touch of Street's skin would pull her, she'd have sheared off the tips of her fingers before she'd lay one on him. Or would she have? Wasn't that the thing about hindsight. Most of the time, it just gave you a blinding headache.

"What's your uncle mixed up in?" Khani closed down the computer and stuffed it into her pack. It wouldn't take much research to uncover Polzin's poison. They'd do it later though. This called for old-school face time.

"I don't know," Isay cried.

"Now, I thought we'd moved past the dishonesty." Street sank the pistol into his holster, and then braced his hands on his knees.

"We have. I'm not lying. I don't know what he's into. All I know is sometimes he has me drop boxes for him and every once in a while me and the boys go rough somebody up."

Maybe Zeke happened upon the Polzin operation and poked around for answers. But her brother was sly enough amateurs like these wouldn't have pegged him. It did add a layer of questions to the mounting pile.

"What's in the boxes?" Khani demanded.

"I don't know." The kid's head jerked back and forth. "He told me a long time ago if I ever looked in one of the boxes the next one would have my head in it. So, I ain't fuckin' looked. Would you?"

"This isn't about me, Isay. It's about you and your uncle's wayward path." She straightened and resumed pacing between the two windows. "Who'd you beat around?"

"Nobodies. Low-lifes." The arch of his thin upper lip revealed the silver caps she'd grown too accustomed to seeing during the first part of his interrogation.

"Lower than you?" she gasped.

"Hey, fuck yo—"

Street's leather boot kicked the recline lever. His big hand pressed into the top of the pleather headrest. The punk reclined in a flash with his mouth agape. Street hovered over the bloke. When Khani expected him to shout he whispered so quietly she strained to hear.

"You know governments spend millions of dollars a year teaching their soldiers how to persuade people to comply with their directives, how to pry information out of them. All they really need to do is put those soldiers in a foster home or two." Street rose to his full height and strode into the kitchen.

"What's he doing?" Isay screamed. "What the fuck's he doing?"

Khani couldn't answer if she wanted to. Her boots suctioned to the floor and refused to move. Her gaze locked on the spot where Street had disappeared. Her brain processed the nugget of information she'd been given about his past. The water ran for a few seconds, and then shut off.

He returned a second later carrying a gallon container of bleach. "If bleach is diluted enough, it doesn't burn the esophagus on the way down. It is hard to get the ratios correct without a measuring cup, and I couldn't find one for all your mess."

Isay thrashed against the tape. Khani's heart sank into her shoes. She imagined Street as a brilliant and beautiful child held down and pumped full of chemicals by an overweight house mum bent on world domination. Only her world consisted of children incapable of fighting back. When she thought about it, maybe she and Zeke hadn't had it so bad. At least they'd had each other. Who did Street have?

The closer Street got to Isay the whiter the boy's clamped lips became. Street set the container on the ground by the chair. He clamped a hand under the boy's clenched jaw and stilled it. His thumb and forefinger pinched Isay's large nose.

"I'm sorry. I'm sorry. I won't cuss her again. Just please don't do that," he begged. Tears poured down his cheek.

"Okay." Street righted the chair. "But I think you need to apologize."

"I'm sorry. I won't cuss you ever again." Isay sucked at the boogers dripping down his lip. His eyes rimmed with red.

"Apology accepted." Khani schooled her gaze on the punk, yet she really wanted to study her unlikely partner. An engine rumbled toward the cockeyed cabin. "Sock him." She moved to the nearest window and watched a shiny granite truck complete with a neon 2015 sticker, wench, and off-road tires, dodge mud puddles as though they brimmed with lava.

A man in hiking pants so crisp they'd never seen a trail stepped out. He slammed the door and sinewy muscles flexed under his extra-medium long sleeves topped with a navy fleece vest. With bounding strides and careful footfalls he maneuvered the worst parts of the slushy yard. The only rugged thing about the man was the leather holster strapped to his hip and the fixed blade protruding from it.

Khani moved to the door. Rapid, heavy stomps on the first step shook the entire house. She pictured him slugging the mud from his pristine Merrell's and a smile flirted with her lips. If he hated mud on his shoes how would he feel about blood on them? When his treads neared she opened the door and stepped into the opening with her hand extended.

"Hi. You must be Vasaya." She let her smile shine. "Isay has told me so much about you."

Light brown eyebrows shot to a buzzed hairline. "Who are you?"

"A recent acquaintance of your nephew's," she purred.

His gaze roved her tight pants and fitted top, and then rewound over her legs. "Sorry. I, ah, wasn't expecting anyone besides my nephew." He wrapped a warm hand around hers and caressed the back with his thumb. "Especially someone so much better suited for a mature audience."

"Oh, your nephew and I aren't acquainted like that." Khani narrowed her gaze, but maintained her smile.

"Even better." Vasaya's grip tightened.

"Isay is tied up at the moment and couldn't get the door. Please, come in. Let's talk." She tugged him forward with an expectant twinkle in her eyes.

"Just talk?" A few feet inside his gaze swung from her. It lit on Street, and then fused to his bound nephew. His eager steps faltered.

"I expect you'll scream a little too." Khani divested him of his blade and slung it into the wall. At the same time, she lifted their clasped hands and twisted clockwise. She clamped onto his presented wrist with her throwing hand. Her thumb pressed his lower limb into an L. She used her freed hand to lock his elbow in place and shove everything against his shoulder blades.

A bellow erupted from his throat.

"See? Screaming." With minimal, well-placed pressure, she drove him to his knees. "You have two choices, Vasaya. Tell me what I want to know or I'll pry it out of you. Just look at Izzy and you can see fighting is valiant, but futile. Besides, we both know you're not the valiant type."

"You'll pay for this, bitch." He lunged forward.

Isay whipped his head in rapid shakes. A suppressed cry erupted from behind the sock.

Khani maintained her hold on the chap's wrist, but released his elbow. He landed on his left hand, his right arm extended behind him. His legs kicked blindly.

Her gaze honed on his protracted arm, specifically his knobby elbow. She cocked her right palm. Khani powered through the joint. A crack ricocheted around the room.

"That's gotta' hurt." Street winced.

She stepped back and allowed his wail to roar without muffling it. Most of the people that lived on the street weren't home. She guessed they wouldn't bother to call the police if they were.

Vasaya cradled his misshaped arm. He balled into the fetal position.

Finally his howling abated to sniveling. Khani leaned over him and stared into his glassy brown eyes. "Why did you order junior to lead Zeke Slaughter into the middle of an ice-field and leave him?"

His gaze livened with a series of blinks. Shrewd brown eyes shifted back and forth between her, Street, and his nephew. He shuddered. "Jesus. Look, I'm small time. A few shipments of coke a year. I'm not in with these guys."

"What guys, Vasaya?" she asked, her interest piqued.

"I don't know," he groaned.

Khani snatched his good hand and flipped him over.

"No. No. Listen," he squealed. "My cousin, Aleksey, lives in New York. He set me up with his supplier to funnel through Alaska. Low risk. Low income. Just enough to help during the long winter."

"But..." Khani offered.

His breaths condensed, misting the dark wooden floor. "A week before this Slaughter guy was due to show for a tour I got a note in the shipment. It said I'd find a quarter million wired into my shadow account for my compliance. If I didn't, I'd find my wife's severed head on my kitchen counter the next day."

"You're married? What a lucky lady," Street interjected.

Khani barely heard the aside. Her brain calculated the meaning of the news. A bigger force worked against her brother than she ever imagined. "What exactly did they order you to do?"

"Usher him to the middle of the ice-field, leave him, and..." A sob shook his torso. "And never speak about it or I'd lose my head."

"I want the note," she demanded.

"I burned it and the picture they included of a man's severed head. An actual head," he hollered.

Khani released his hand. "When you brought him to the ice-fields, how'd you know where the middle was? It's an expansive place."

He rolled onto his back and shielded his crooked arm with his good one. Dirt smeared the front of his vest and his white sleeves. "They gave coordinates," he sniveled. "Latitude and longitude. It took forever to figure out the actual location. I'm a businessman, not a militant or boy scout. Heck, I've only been on the neatly paved paths that run in front of the glacier and that was for a photo shoot."

Vasaya had a point. Only boy scouts, pilots, sailors, and militants used specific coordinates. Her gaze met Street's. From the look in his eyes he thought the same thing, and it didn't bode well for her brother.

Chapter Eleven

He strummed the keyboard. After a few passwords and a fingerprint scan, Street searched the Base Branch database for Vasaya Polzin. It pulled information from every national and international database that knowing or unwittingly allowed them access. In seconds he had the bloke's tax returns for the last decade, bank accounts, real estate, email and social media profiles ready to be accessed in the fancy dashboard. A few more pecks had some high level software decrypting the wire transfer into Vasaya's account and tracing it to the source.

It had taken precious time to secure the Polzins in the local precinct in solitary confinement until further notice. Well, time, plus two faux FBI badges and a call to the "Director of the FBI", which actually led them to Vail's cell phone. Luckily the chappie knew how to work off the cuff. It had also taken the proper amount of leverage with the knowledge that members of their force had taken bribes from at least one person over the last year. They'd burned a bit of daylight, but they couldn't have either of the bastards blabbing about their interrogation. Not until after they found Khani's brother.

Street leaned back from the small hotel desk while the computer did its thing. He threaded his hands behind his neck. Across from him, slender fingers clacked frantically on the keys of her laptop.

"Are we going to talk about this?"

"There's nothing to talk about," she snapped. "We don't know anything yet."

"We know more than we knew this morning."

"And I don't like it any better because Zeke isn't sitting in front of me."

"I'm sitting in front of you. I'm trying to help you, but I can't do that if you won't trust me."

Her bruised knuckles hovered over the letters. She shouldn't have punched the wall at Isay's. It showed a lack of control that might cost them in a head-down, balls-tucked situation, and yet, at the same time it showed a level of humanity he'd never expected from her rigidity.

At long last, the leaden striations or her eyes shimmered in his direction. "I'm activating a tracker I put in Zeke's wallet before he left for the States."

His fingers slowly unthreaded and fell to his sides. "You had a tracker on him and you're just now activating the thing?"

"It was in case of emergencies only."

"And your brother missing in Alaska wasn't an emergency?" He shrugged. "You came here looking for him." His mouth hung open for a minute and he inhaled her scent across his tongue. "I don't understand."

She ticked away on her laptop. "I wouldn't expect you to."

"If you won't even try and explain it, how can I?"

Her chest rose and fell on an exaggerated huff. "I don't need to explain myself to you."

He held his tongue and her gaze.

"Zeke put a tracker on my car three years ago. When I found it I didn't speak to him for a year."

His brow quirked in question.

"It's not the fact that it was there. It's the fact that he didn't ask my permission or even tell me when he put it there. We've been through hell together. We tell each other everything. He's the only person I trust completely and he broke that trust."

"He did it to keep you safe."

"Doesn't matter. Once it's broken you can never really get it back. You can try, but it's not the same."

"So you put a tracker on him out of spite?"

"No. After we started talking again—"

"You mean after you started talking to him again?"

She slammed back into the chair. "Yes. Okay? When I started talking to him again. We agreed to have trackers on each other as a safety net, used only in the case of extreme emergencies." One of her shoulders bobbed. "I had to be sure."

"You are an interesting creature, Khani Slaughter."

"You can't tell me trust comes easily for you? Not after what you said at Polzin's."

"Since when am I a fan of easy?"

After a pile of seconds her gaze dropped and she plunked on the computer again. Street watched the gears work their magic on his end.

"I think it's about time you tell me exactly what you know about your brother's hobbies." He didn't tack on his, 'because this doesn't look good,' opinion to the end.

She clamped her mouth shut and considered him for so long he thought she might never speak again. "He works for a US-based private security firm."

"Private securities, a.k.a. guns for hire?" She loved her brother despite his shoddy moral compass. Yet, she treated him like an airborne strain of the plague. Street shook his head. "And I'm the bad guy."

"You're not the bad guy. I'm the bad girl." Khani looked away and toiled with the zipper on her jacket. When she'd stepped foot in his room she'd refused to take the thing off, wearing it like a coat of armor.

Street's gaze centered the screen and the completed diagnostic. His fists clenched. "Grisha Filipov." He tested the name on his tongue, hoping it wasn't the same Grisha about whom he'd heard tales wicked enough to keep him up at night.

"No." Khani's hands flew to her mouth.

Damn. It was.

Apparently she'd heard a horror or two about the man. He thought to wrap her in his arms, to protect her from this, but it wouldn't give her comfort. The only way for him to help her was by finding her brother.

"Work on your tracker, Khani. I'll research Filipov and see what I can find."

She nodded, her gaze far off in some version of possible outcome for this nightmare. That in itself, his trooper, the fiercest person he knew glassed over and near catatonic, had his fingers striking the keys at lightning speed.

Only he didn't research Filipov. He knew all he needed to know about the monster. He harkened to the file hidden on his hard-drive labeled Slaughter. It opened to two files Zeke and Khani. He never touched the latter, knowing it would breach a trust he needed to earn. He'd only riffled through Zeke's enough to know what the bloke looked like, his current address, and his former employment history. Street had purposefully steered clear of the US Elite file under the bloke's name.

US Elite was a private security firm. Though he'd tried not to jump to conclusions, he'd guessed Zeke had moved to the States to contract for them. There had been a possibility he'd been ordered to infiltrate their ranks for Queen and Country, or hell, even the Base Branch. They dealt in covert ops, which sometimes meant, unless you were on the top tier of power, one team didn't know the tasks another was commissioned to do. Heck, when he'd made LTC he'd found out about three units under the London command he hadn't known existed. Surely there could've been more. But if Khani didn't even know about it, chances were good Zeke had turned his back on his ethics and now worked for the almighty pound or dollar, as it were.

He clicked on the US Elite file and scanned its contents. Most recently Zeke had been ordered to penetrate the New York associate of the Stas, the Russian mob named for its leader Lev Stas. The man's reputation preceded him the world over.

Access to the Queen's clearance codes worked to his advantage quite often, opening doors otherwise unyielding. Street clicked through a manifest and mission plan he shouldn't have. The company had been contracted by an anonymous source the same day a small Russian nuclear warhead became a supposed item on the black market's most exclusive auction block.

"I've got him." The legs of Khani's chair scraped across the floor. She shot up from the chair. "We have to add to our packs. Sleeping bags, more food, and way more ammo."

Street closed his laptop and stood. "Where is it?"

"He," she corrected. "On a mountain ridge a little past the coordinates where Isay left him." Khani slammed the laptop closed and shoved it in her small pack. "Get ready. If we leave in twenty we should be able to make it halfway to the pass before nightfall. It'll take us the rest of the night to make it to the beacon, but we'll reach it by daylight." She slung the bag onto her shoulder. "Meet downstairs in fifteen."

Apprehension leaked from her pores, but he knew she'd die before she gave voice to it. Khani rounded the table, leaving him staring at an ugly print of an uglier acrylic painting of a maroon flower. She brushed past, headed for the door behind him, the scent of her fear strong in the air.

His hand snaked out and latched onto her wrist, nearly wrapping his fingers around her thin bones twice. She stretched his arm so far back he thought she'd take it with her, but she finally stopped. He held perfectly still, prepared to take the brunt of an attack without blinking. "Isay left him nine days ago."

Her wrist jerked. Street lowered his eyes, tuning into his other senses since he couldn't see her. The air around them stiffened. She held her breath.

"If Zeke were able and unrestricted," he continued, "he'd have marched himself off that glacier, found the kid, and pounded him into the pavement for ditching him, or he'd have explored on his own and made it back in time to call you."

"He might be injured, taking shelter in a cave. You don't know he's not there," she argued.

"I'm not saying we shouldn't go. We should and we are, but we can't kill ourselves trying to get there by dawn. We'll do him no good dead. You need to step back and look at this dispassionately." Street released her wrist, and then slid his fingers across the heel of her palm. He pressed slowly. She un-balled her fist, allowing him to thread their fingers.

"I don't think I can be dispassionate about this anymore. It's too close to my heart," she whispered.

Did she only mean the deal with her brother?

"Then let me help you."

She slipped her fingers from his hold. Her steps retreated. The door opened. When it should have shut it didn't. He waited, his heart knocking.

"Okay," she said, and then the door latched and she was gone.

Street sat, opened the computer, and read.

Three members of Elite's security force had been assigned to permeate Stas from different angles. Zeke had been tasked to become a member of the security detail. A hacker named Derrick Coen had been charged with aiding his acceptance, tracking their moves, and trying to trace the warhead. A woman, Greer Britton, had been loaded with gaining access by enticing the upper-level Stas by any and all means necessary.

His stomach churned. *What assholes.*

With a couple of clicks he opened two other dashboards for more information on Greer Britton and Derrick Coen. Both were reported missing two days ago.

Chapter Twelve

Khani fancied herself impervious to annoying sounds. When Zeke had been a kid he'd steadily built her tolerance for incessant mouth farts and machine gun fire, sirens, and even foul-mouthed rants. The relentless crunch of ice under her boots, however, shaved a layer off her frazzled nerve endings one step at a time. Multiply that by four determined feet and she considered throwing herself down the next ravine they skirted.

"Talk about something?" she begged. Street had been mummy quiet since they'd left the hotel. His silence had given her time to assimilate to the situation at hand and shift to mission mode. For that she'd been grateful.

Now the sun hung low in the sky. The peak they sought took one step away for every one they steadied toward it. Intermittently, swirls of blue marbled in the ice. White, shades of drab, and deeply shadowed black stretched as far as her field of vision. Thick fog mimicked her mood, hanging low and dire.

"Nice ass."

Her snorted laugh echoed off the sheer slab of ice on their right and tickled her even more. She continued up the incline, painfully aware of the heat increasing between her thighs. At least it fended off the cold. At most it made a detour into Street's pants, which was too inviting a possibility for her own good. "You say nothing for nearly six hours, and that's what you open with?"

"Why do you think I haven't said anything since we started? I've been staring at your perfectly-formed keister jostling about. When that thing's distracting a bloke there's not room for intellectual conversation. I could tell you all the ways I've thought about touching it, kissing it, penetrating it."

Khani's chest flushed so hot she feared she might give off steam. She jerked to a halt.

"You thinking about giving any of those a go?" He laughed.

But damn it, she wasn't laughing. There was no room for laughter between fear and lust. "You take the lead," she muttered.

"Last time I tried that you didn't like it and I ended up taped to a chair. Not that I'm complaining." His boots crunched the ice until they pulled even with hers. A lopsided grin quirked his face.

"Just get in front of me."

"Oh, you fancy a look at my rear, troop?" He winked. "Still not complaining. You might though. I have kind of a big arse for a chap." His powerful legs pulled ahead with ease.

At least his round cheeks and thick thighs gave her something else to think about besides her missing brother and the never-ending iceberg. It didn't do much for her restraint though. She fought the insane urge to unbuckle his pants, shove them down to his knees, and spank his smooth cheeks with her open hand. Again and again. Until he begged her to straddle his hips and ride the orgasm out of him.

They marched on for an hour and a half with her fantasizing about his body in various compromised positions with a diverse assortment of bonds. She pulled off another layer so she wouldn't break out in a sweat from her mental adventure—it was more exerting than the physical one.

Street cocked his head over his shoulder. "It's that good, huh?"

"Yep," she admitted, unable to deny the I-want-to-fuck-you look staining her face.

"I aim to please." He hiked another few hundred yards, and then pointed at a black spot in the mountain face. "It'll be pitch soon. I say we huddle into that shallow outcrop and get some sleep. You need it for tomorrow. We don't really know what we're up against yet. I could use some too."

"As long as nothing else has claimed it first."

They picked up the pace and made it to the shallow cave, though calling it a cave stretched the meaning of the word. It looked more like a pothole in the side of the steep rock formation.

"Looks like you don't have to run from a grizzly…today."

"Silver linings, I guess."

"After you, my lady." He used a formal Brit accent, extended his left arm, crossed the other over his middle, and bowed low.

She yanked the knitted wool cap off his head as she tucked into the low, reaching space. The ground level stretched probably twelve feet long and about five feet deep. A jagged ceiling hung at her eye level at the entrance, but gradually tapered until she decided to shuck her pack and sit in the far corner.

Street scrubbed his stubbly head several times, and then crawled into the opening. His bulk sucked up the space and all the free freezing air with it.

Her lungs seized. She scrambled to her knees embarrassed and completely unable to stop the anxiety attack that bore on her without warning. She'd been so comfortable around him. So at ease. Too at ease that she'd dropped her guard, the one she constantly adjusted and repositioned to keep anyone from knowing that being trapped in a small space with a man was enough to kill her.

"What's your call sign, Slaughter?" He barked in command.

Her vision tunneled to his face, but some autonomic system in her brain powered by years of training took over. She heard her raspy voice say, "Lima. Echo. Oscar. Papa. Alfa. Romeo. Delta. One. Nine. Nine. Four."

"Height?"

She syphoned a breath. "Five-eleven."

"Weight?"

"One-thirty-seven." Her throat quit convulsing and she swallowed past the dryness. "You're not supposed to ask a woman how much she weights."

Street smiled and leaned his back against the rock wall. "Welcome back."

Khani collapsed onto her heels and let her clenched fists fall into her lap. Now that she could breathe her chest rose and fell in mad waves. A plastic canteen entered the field of her lowered gaze.

"Drink a little. It'll help with the head ache."

She swallowed a few sips and returned the container. "How'd you know what to do? Only two people have ever seen me freak and both tried coddling me." Her teeth scrapped across her bottom lip. "It didn't go over well."

"A kid in one of the foster homes used to get panic attacks. It helped curve the worst of it if he recited inane facts. Multiplication tables. The periodic table."

"Smart kid. The boys I knew could only recite the names of the players in their favorite football club."

"Sometimes, if it didn't subside after the others, I got to that."

Her gaze lifted to his green eyes and easy expression. "Do you ever feel like the world is shrinking in on you these days?"

"No. Not in a long time." He shed his pack, took a long swig, and then stashed the water inside. "My world keeps growing."

"I moved to a different country, across an ocean, and sometimes it's not enough."

"The question..." Street stopped, seemed to toy with the words, discard them, and then chuck the new ones. He yanked his sleeping bag from the bottom zipper of his pack, and then eyed her. "The question is, what's tying you to the past?" His stubbled chin waggled. "You figure that out, and then confront it or set it free."

Khani considered the answer to that question so attentively that until the zipper of her sleeping bag whined open she didn't notice Street had retrieved it from her bag. She wiped at her frosty nose with the back of her gloved hand. "Thanks."

"No problem. Can I have my hat back? I'm freezing my nuts off over here." His torso disappeared into a puffy winter-camo cocoon, the bottom of which thrashed around as he rubbed his feet together so fast he might start a fire.

She grinned and tossed over his hat. "If you say we could snuggle to stay warm, I'll punch you."

"Nah. I was just thinking how good a sewer vent would feel right about now."

He'd threatened to check up on Zeke if she didn't talk. Had he? And if he did, what did he know about her past? Her headache, incited by the panic attack, charged back to life, ramming her forehead dead center. The impact rippled across to her temples. Did he know she'd spent too many nights to count huddled next to steam vents, her body wrapped around Zeke's more susceptible one, trying to stave off **pneumonia**? Did he know how often she'd prayed for a foster home? Punishments or not, didn't he know how lucky he was?

"Do you think that's funny?" she bit.

"No." He tossed back the top of her bag and motioned her inside. "I think it's smelly as fuck, but damn warm when you're soaked to the bone in thirty-eight degrees and you haven't seen the sunlight in months." When she stayed frozen the icy rock of his gloved hand wrapped her wrist once again and tugged her forward. "Get in before your lips turn blue."

Khani tucked her feet into the stuffed nylon, boots and all. She levered her bottom up and wiggled her legs and hips in as well. Warmth collected around her ankles and seeped through her pants, warding off the chill. The position of the sleeping bag had her as close to Street as she'd been on this trip with the exception of the kiss.

She swallowed past the warring emotion he knotted in her throat. "How do you know that?"

Tiny lines crinkled around the corners of his eyes. "Firsthand experience, winter of ninety-five and the five after."

She probably flashed the not-so-rookie more defined lines on their way to wrinkles, but she couldn't care about that. The shock of what he said resonated. "You would have been seven years old then."

He chuckled. "Eight and a half. The first winter after I told my fourth foster mum to shove it."

"Bloody fucking Christ." She poked her fingers into her beanie, and then tugged at the hair at her nape. A force she hadn't experienced in a long time swept over her. It weighed a thousand tons and made her want to collapse onto the floor. Helplessness. It zapped her energy and her ability to hold up the wall she'd erected around herself for so very long. Because Street—as much as she—knew the fear and inferiority of being an unkept child.

"Zeke was twelve when we split. I was sixteen. We barely survived and we had each other." She didn't complete the thought. He was smart enough to figure it out anyway.

"You had someone to count on," he nodded. "You also had someone to hold you back."

Every fiber in her being wanted to deny his words. She'd only whispered them in her head once. It was the weekend. No school. They'd gone without a meal for two days. Things looked so bleak. The sinister thought scribbled itself on a tiny corner of her brain. Guilt had forced her to eat only half of her food at school and save the rest for the following weekend and everyone after. That way she'd never think those awful things about the only person in the world who loved her.

"It was probably easier for me. I didn't have anyone on my shoulders."

"Or in your corner," Khani added.

"Not for a long time, but then…" The sage of his soulful eyes cast to the uneven rock above, without really seeing it. His inspection turned inward for the briefest of seconds. "But then, Father Tommy took a scrapper under his wing, tutored me, and threatened me with the eternal pits of hell, if I didn't quit pissin' my smarts away." A faint smile rounded his lips. "His words, not mine."

The territory on which she treaded was rugged and unfamiliar, but she stepped anyway. "What about your parents?"

His expelled breath drifted over her neck. One thick brow hiked. "What about your parents?" he asked in a whisper.

All the bravery that had fortified her moments ago vanished. Her open mouth clamped shut and refused even the air in her lungs passage. Why was it so hard to talk about them? They'd haunted her childhood. Why did she hold on to the terror to this day?

Because she knew no other way.

Khani reclined onto the unforgiving ground. She tucked her head into the mummy top and cinched the zipper tight. The roughened ceiling faded with the sunlight. A minute passed in total silence, but for the wind howling at the entrance.

At her left fabric rustled. Then cold silence took hold.

How close they'd been to... What? Honesty. A connection. As much as her heart ached ... it was how things had always been. Lone. Cool. Detached. Save for her brother's love and her love for him. She clutched a fist to her chest and covered it with her other hand. Sleep hounded her heels, but refused to make the kill.

"A bartender heading home from work found me swaddled in a blanket inside a cardboard box on the corner of Studland and King Street."

She compounded her grip, hugging herself hard enough to steady the heart quaking her entire chest. Desire willed her to wrap him in her arms and hold him tight. Khani rolled, facing the back of the cave, and huddled into the bag. She cursed Street's cunt of a mother for abandoning him. She cursed him for making her love him. She cursed herself for being too chicken-shit—as Tyler often said—to confide in him.

Khani forced her breaths to steady and low, mimicking the sleep that would surely not take her tonight. The blackness she stared into became the promise of her future, one she'd never given much thought to, one that suddenly looked eerily bleak.

Minutes passed. They morphed into an hour, and then two. Street's breathing grew long and deep. When she felt certain he couldn't fake the easy snores rumbling in his chest she twisted to face him.

The outline of his forehead, nose, and strong jaw were darker than the grey night beyond. A peace eased the beat of her heart. Whether it was him or the moonlight filtering in, this perspective seemed so much brighter than the solitary back of the cave.

She pillowed her head on her left arm and reached her right outside the envelope of heat the nylon, cotton, and her body created. The icy air prickled the gap that formed between her glove and sleeve. Carefully she lowered her arm around Street's billowy sleeping bag and held him close.

His chest rose and then settled in a contented breath. She got lost in the rhythm of his breathing and slipped into the sweet oblivion of sleep.

Chapter Thirteen

Street hadn't slept that well ever. That said something. He slept like a brick anywhere. Did it make him a total fanny that the tiny arm of a sexy woman he'd grown to adore worked as the best tonic in the land? Probably—and he didn't give a shit. He didn't even care that when he'd yawned like a bear she'd snatched it away as though he might've bitten it off.

He stepped back into the cave after relieving himself. Both their bags sat propped against the rock wall, sleeping bags, protein bar packages, and water nowhere in sight. "You've been busy."

Khani leaned again the cave next to her pack, her knees tucked under her chin, arms around her legs in a self-comforting position. She seemed so vulnerable. Closed off, and yet, open at the same time. He'd never seen her anything but on point, which meant on guard. Slowly, a millimeter at a time, she revealed her secrets.

"I want to make it to the beacon in time to plan our next move and execute before nightfall." She tugged the cap lower on her ears and stood as much as the shelter allowed.

There it was again, a tiny acknowledgement that she'd actually listened to what he'd said. He lifted her pack and she slipped into it without a fuss. His gaze snagged on the silky hair that slid across his bare fingers. He clamped his eyes shut against the hunger that threatened to buckle his knees.

Street cleared his throat. "That shouldn't be hard. It's barely light outside, but enough we won't break our necks." He stepped back, hefted his pack, and then stepped into the serenity of dawn on a glacier.

They settled into a fast pace with Khani in the lead. Every few hundred yards or so she checked the map and tracker strength, making certain they stayed on course. Street watched the tree line growing to their right and the ridge on their left. If anyone wanted to pick them off, this was the place. They were balls-out exposed. It rankled the hairs on his nape, but there was nothing to be done about it except keep moving.

She did. One foot in front of the other, Khani pushed the tempo. The closer they drew to the pulse of Zeke's tracker the faster her heels shoved off the crisp ice. Street sensed her reserves slipping.

Four hours after they started hiking, the grade finally flattened and packed snow added a layer of irritation to the hike.

"I can't believe you two were going to do this for fun."

"Me either." She stopped abruptly and stabbed the air. "Look." The sun crowned the first of four knobby mountains in the distance. Hints of blue sky peeked through puffy white clouds while spindly rays of light glistened off every surface. Were they not standing in the middle of it, the picture would've been idyllic. Her aim centered the nearest ridge. "The beacon is coming from the base of that first formation."

Her face angled in his direction. Sweat shined on her upper lip. Street caught her arm. "Wait." He clamped the end of his glove between his teeth and yanked it off. As though taming a wild animal he moved his hand steadily toward her face while maintaining eye contact.

The zipper-pull of her jacket flapped with her rapid breaths. Cold skin greeted his warm. He swiped the moisture off her mouth with his thumb, and then licked it off the pad of his finger. "You need to slow down. I know it's hard, but if you sweat through your clothes, I'll be forced to strip you, and warm you with my body." He released her. "We can't have you succumbing to hypothermia."

"No," she breathed, "we can't. You lead for a while. I won't be able to pace myself." Her petite red nose shined against her pale face.

Street's gaze sharpened on the spot where he'd rubbed away sweat, and apparently, make-up. Tiny scars, almost translucent in the daylight, criss-crossed her skin in a random pattern. Her hand flew to her mouth. His gaze leapt to her wide one.

She dropped her hand, and the action looked like it cost her. "Later, okay?"

"Later." He nodded, stepped around her, and pushed forward, knowing those scars had something to do with the reason she walled the world off and wondering why. Surely it wasn't their appearance. They were barely noticeable in the best light and not at all with her cosmetics obsession. Which meant it had to do with receiving the scars and the ones the experience left on her insides.

Oh Khani, how fucked up we are.

The powder thickened the farther they climbed, bogging his big boots. He glanced over his shoulder and found Khani walking literally in his footsteps.

"Quit smiling at me," she commanded. "It's easier. This way."

"Sure, make me do all the work."

"If you were pounding one out, you wouldn't be complaining, would you?"

"Nope. But that's not work, now is it?"

"No." She shooed him on with her hands. "Now move it."

Street did his best to keep a pace steady enough to hedge their heart rates, but also fast enough to keep her from stomping him into the snow. As soon as they reached the narrow shadow of the mountain Khani passed him.

Desperation propelled her into a sprint. It was all he could do to keep his arse upright and her from leaving him in the flurries of her pursuit.

She bailed from her pack ten yards from the outcropping. "Zeke," she bellowed. Black hair whipped left and right in her desperate attempt to locate her brother, despite her earlier words. Her shoulders lowered and she cleared the distance in seconds. "Zeke!"

Khani dove into the snow knees first. Her arms wind-milled. White sailed behind her. All around her. The tip of a large black boot shown horizontal to her frantic form.

Street's heart crawled up his chest cavity.

Please God, don't let her have come all this way to find him buried in the snow.

He ditched his pack and raced to her side. Street plowed so much snow with his abrupt stop his knees hit the ice underneath. His hands poised to free Zeke's body from the frozen earth. He stilled beside Khani and stared down.

A large man in black cargo pants and hiking boots lay face-down in the snow. Frozen blood clotted brown hair. A tattoo on his partially obscured forearm read, 'Sinner' in Russian Cyrillic script. SOS stained the man's wrist. It didn't add up.

Zeke Slaghter's military profile only referenced one tattoo. A dagger, the logo for the Royal Marine Commandos, ran up his abdomen, over his left pectoral, and stopped at his heart. Unless he'd gotten the Russian ink long ago and showered in the barracks fully clothed, there was no way he could have hidden them in Her Majesty's Royal Marines.

Khani roared and gnashed at the snow, her face a mask of rage and disbelief. Her arms gouged at the powder with frantic pulls.

"Stop. Khani." Street reached out to still her. Her elbow shot out and found the center of his solar plexus. His thumb rubbed at the sting. He choked out, "It's not him."

She continued to dig like a woman possessed.

He used his shoulder and drove it into her, bowling her over. Her head sank into the snow inches from the dead man's shoulder. Street's legs pinned hers to the ground. His arms knotted hers between their chests.

The heat of her screams blasted his cheek. She thrashed beneath him, her entire body rigid.

"Spasite Ot Syda," he yelled.

She stilled. Her eyes finally focused on him. "What?"

"Save me from judgment. It's the tattoo on the bloke's wrist."

"What?" she sobbed the word. Her bottom lip quivered.

"That body has at least two Russian mob tats. That isn't your brother, not unless he affiliated ten or more years ago without you knowing. The ink is old."

Her gaze cut to the body. No longer fearing her flying fists, he sat back and pulled her up to her knees again. She braced her hands in the snow and panted. The heat of her breaths curled into the day.

He leaned around her and moved the snow off the man's arm. A cry seeped from her lips. She hung her head between her shoulder blades and yelled, covering her sorrow and relief in rage. The piercing sound faded into the wind.

Street grabbed the man's belt and flipped him onto his back. A scar ran the length of his face, pulling down the edge of his right eye. He reached into the dead man's pockets. A set of keys filled the right front and a wallet barely fit inside the front left.

The American license of Zeke Slaughter occupied the first flap of the black leather trifold. No surprise there. They'd probably hoped the body would remain forever hidden in the ice field, but should it surface due to scavenging they'd covered their bases. Amateurs. They hadn't even fastened the belt around his waist or put the jacket tucked beneath the body on him.

Trenched and mussed snow surrounded the body aside from the mess Khani had created. Beyond the line they'd travelled to get here the snow turned to hard packed ice. No discernible path led to or away from the scene, besides theirs.

"I don't think Zeke killed him." She settled onto her heels, and then stood. Her head turned this way and that, taking in the scene.

"Me neither. There are at least six different prints around the body. They probably ambushed him at night and left this lucky bachelor in his place."

"Damnit." Khani yanked the crooked beanie from her head and tugged at her hair.

"This is a good thing. They want information from Zeke otherwise he'd be the one laying in the snow with a hole in the back of his head."

She pulled back on the cap, and then shook her hands out like a fighter getting loose before a match. "Okay. You're right. They want information. He won't give it. They'll torture him." She said it with trained distance. "They'll need a place to do it. Some place quiet and out of the way." Khani spun on her heels with her arms wide. "So where the fuck would they take him from here? They didn't leave tracks."

Street walked downhill to his pack, and then carried it to the rock ledge. He hauled the laptop from the recesses. "I'll redirect an infrared satellite to scan the surrounding area. Your brother is a big chap and this is the middle of freaking nowhere. They couldn't have gone far. You get ahold of Tucker and give him a heads-up. You'll want extraction, if not help on the ground." He set the satellite to work with a few clicks.

"Oh, I don't want help on the ground. I want every last one of them for myself."

"Well, tough shit, troop. I'm taking my fair share."

"He's *my* brother."

"And you're..." He bit his tongue. If he finished that sentence with you're-my-*anything*, he'd obliterate all the headway he'd made. Though hadn't he already? Yes, if she ever found out he looked into her brother's affairs. "...wasting time. Go make the call."

The heat signature came back with three possible structures. One sat directly north of them, another to the east, and the last to the west. The northern one was closest, and therefore the most logical, but he eased back literally and figuratively. He thought about what he'd learned about the Russian mob and Zeke in the fifteen minutes Khani had given him alone at the hotel.

Top was the head, the leader. Right was the heir to the throne. Left was the enforcer. They divided territories in this convoluted method. A low ranking member of the organization lived south of the heir and the killer, who lived equidistant west and east of their leader, whose home was always north.

Isay and his uncle were south. Stas was north. Which meant in this complicated mess, Grisha would set-up in the west—available or not— he'd make it so.

Street plotted the coordinates on his map, and then stashed the computer in his pack. Khani stood near her bag, hip cocked, one hand on the sway of her waist, and the other on the phone.

He plotted their course and then studied the landforms around their target. A swath of deep crevices yawned between them and the cabin. That, and a shit ton of miles. The structure sat high on the incline of the glacier-fed river with a steep drop down the back to the water below. A small shed stood to the south of the main building. One winding road led in and out of the place. They couldn't make it easy, could they?

With the advance plotted, Street folded the map, and then stuffed it into the pocket on his thigh. He used his boots and shoved loose snow over the body. When it looked like no more than a heap he walked a little way from the scene toward the west, hoping to find some reassurance he wasn't leading them down the wrong path.

Twice his feet slipped on the incline and slick surface. The third time did him in. Hard and fast the ice met his keister with a smack. He laid on his pack and glared at the sleek shell of frozen water. From the intimate slant, Street noticed more than thirty distinct boot prints. They gouged the roughened ice, leaving behind glossy patches that made walking difficult at best.

"Laying down on the job, King?" Khani extended her hand.

Maybe he'd hit his head on the fall. She'd called him by his given name. His gaze jumped to her face. All the misery that had carved her features with sharp lines had softened into...hope, and something else. He'd seen Khani wide-eyed twice: once in shock at seeing him in DC and once in excitement at his willingness to submit. He'd never seen her smokey gaze wide with what he could only call wonderment. He looked behind him, expecting to see Zeke strolling from the tree line. But only they were crazy enough to be this far up the Alaskan glacier during the melting season.

"I found tracks," he said dumbly.

"Then let's follow them." She wiggled her protracted hand.

It would be safer for him to peel himself off the ice than it would be to accept her hand. But Khani hadn't made the offer casually. She made it with intent and a meaning that maxed-out every blood vessel in his body.

Street pulled off his right glove. He wrapped his naked palm around Khani's. "Yes, ma'am."

She tugged him up without incident, unless he counted the toe-to-toe stare-off in which they tangled. Lust and her delicious mouth charmed his gaze south. He strained every fibrous grain of his self-control and poured himself into her weighted admiration.

"Thank you," she breathed.

He wouldn't ask for what. It didn't matter. She'd dropped another notch of her steel wall, allowed him to peek over the top. "Always." He nodded and granted her the lead with a tilt of his head.

"Your find, your lead."

"You just want to stare at my bum, huh?" Street held both arms out like an airplane and negotiated the slick path toward the brush.

"That's just a bonus. I want you to clear the path through that mess."

He didn't have to see her to know she likely stabbed a finger and rolled her eyes at the waist high, tightly-woven bushes fringing the forest head. "If five guys—one of them not going willingly—dozed through there even a week and a half ago, they did the worst part for us. And if there's not a path, we know they didn't go that way."

"True."

"What did Vail say?" Street maintained an easy pace on the hazardous path and Khani stayed on his six.

"He has a friend at Elmendorf-Richardson in Anchorage who owes him a favor."

"What are they going to do? Write our last will and testament?"

"It's a joint military base, not a law office. They'll send a bird to get us whenever, wherever."

"We'll find him, Khani. I can't guarantee what shape he'll be in after a week, but we'll find him."

Street stepped over a narrow gap in the ice and came face to face with infinity. "Blow me." White ice swirled with blue, turning brighter and brighter in color the deeper it went. The skinny chasm went deep enough that his balls tucked close to his body for fear of dropping in and never being recovered.

"Is that an invitation?" Khani laughed. The jolly noise died abruptly. She stepped across the cleft, cleared a safe distance, and then leaned over the edge and peered down. "Give me a jungle, desert, or city any day of the week. This shit creeps me out."

He crossed and yanked a rope from his pack. After a few twists and a tug he created a slipknot, and then held the loop low for Khani to step into. "If that creeps you out, the ones you can't see are sure to make you piss your pants."

Chapter Fourteen

Khani wrestled with the last strap on her shoe-claw things. "Why do we need these things? We didn't need them for the last three."

"They're called crampons."

"I don't give a shit. If I could use them to stomp someone to death, they'd be cool and maybe I'd care, but now." She shook her head. "Nope."

"This soldier is a little bit wider than the rest, wouldn't you say?"

Street stood at the edge of a precipice too wide to cross with an adrenaline-fueled leap as they'd done before. It was also so long they couldn't see either end of it, if it ever ended. He held an ice pick over his head and sucked in a deep breath.

She scrambled to her feet. "Wait a minute," she shrieked. "Aren't there ropes—as in plural—and carabiners and ladders and helmets and harnesses involved in this too?"

"Yep, supposed to be. But we're not Sherpas or professional climbers."

"What the hell is a Sherpa?"

Before she completed her sentence Street threw himself toward death. His arms arched. His torso stretched. The metal points of his crampons nearly pierced his wide, firm butt. Then he crunched, turning all those nylon-covered muscles onto the sheet of ice. The gleaming point of the axe pierced the ice. It hacked shards of crystalline water into the air. The spiny tips of his crampons serrated the wall. Then gravity took hold.

Like a magnet tossed onto the side of a refrigerator, he hit the side of the glacier and slid. Khani's eyes followed the line of rope from his waist, across the dark chasm, and to the other ice pick sticking out of the glacier that the rope looped and knotted. Was it enough to hold him? Was she strong enough to pull him out?

She sat and braced her heels on either side of the axe. Her hands encircled the cross of the blade points to offer reinforcement to the anchor he'd established before leaping. She found him still sliding toward the nothingness.

"King!" She screeched his name, unable to stop herself.

He dug into the wall. A grunt gave voice to the effort it took to slow his decent. Finally his feet stuck more than ten feet from where he'd landed. The rope pressed into the ice on Khani's side of the fissure.

One foot at a time, Street crawled up the wall. He reposted the axe, and then repeated the process. After five excruciating minutes, he heaved himself onto the frozen shelf.

Khani collapsed, her relief more clear than his own, but she didn't care. The ice chilled her and again she didn't care.

After several still minutes save for the rise and fall of his chest—and hers—Street hoisted himself to his feet. "I'll tell you what a Sherpa is when you join me," he echoed across the expanse.

"I don't want to know anymore," she hollered from the ground.

"Make the leap, Khani, and I'll let you kiss me."

She propped onto her elbows. "If I make this leap, it better earn me way more than a kiss."

He spread his arms wide. "Anything you want. Come and get it."

Well, how badly did she want King Street? Or her brother for that matter?

Khani's panted breaths roared in her ears. Her heart rammed into her sternum and the back of her ribs like a crash-test-dummy. She'd faced down cold-blooded killers, land mines, and her abusive father. Could she do this?

"Hell, yes." She stood, cleaved the axe from the ice, and loosened the rope. One quaking foot after the other, she stepped into the circle. The rope cinched around her waist. Her fingers wrapped around the handle of the pick.

She ran for all she was worth, and then leapt into the abyss.

Pick first. Feet second. Pick first. Feet second.

A bloody image of her landing on the sharpened tool flashed in her mind. Then it passed. The ice came fast. The landing came hard. It knocked the little bit of breath she had in her lungs out through a trap door. She held fast.

When oxygen filled her chest again she climbed one claw at a time to the top. King's arms encompassed her. He tugged her against his chest. Her feet dangled in the nothingness, but her heart dangled near the most dangerous cliff of all. Fucking love.

His mouth sealed around hers and stole what little oxygen she'd managed to gain. The axe slipped from her grasp and she clung to him with all her remaining strength. She slipped her tongue inside his mouth and he let her take the lead.

The whip of the wind stung her cheeks, but the security of his hold and the eagerness of his response voided the cold. She wrapped her legs around him, eager for the contact.

He jerked away and gripped her ankles. "I'm all for being your whipping boy, but can we start small with spurs or something? Crampons in the arse might be fatal out here."

"Oh shit." She lowered her leg to the ground. "Did I hurt you?"

"No, but a quarter inch and you'd have left your mark."

Boy, that though erased all the anxiety she'd had about the terrain. She'd like to leave a mark on him all right. A thick leather collar with two handles for her to hold while she rode him sounded like a great place to start. Too bad they were thousands of miles from her toys and too many away from central heat.

"Then we'll save the marking for later."

King blinked.

"I promise to make it much less invasive." She drew an X over her heart. "Promise."

"In that case, let's get a move on. The faster we get Zeke, the faster we can get out of here."

"Lead the way," she said.

They traipsed across two more narrow slits in the ice and made it to the edge of the brush by ten o'clock. King stopped. "You hungry?"

"Always."

He dug what remained of their MREs from the previous day out of her pack and handed hers over. She couldn't hold back the groan. The bean and rice burrito she'd attempted to eat two years ago almost chipped her tooth. She'd opted to eat the individually wrapped sides and dessert yesterday and save the worst for last.

"Come on, it's not that bad."

"Easy for you to say. You drew a ham slice." Khan rolled her eyes to the sky. "Why you didn't scarf it already is beyond me." She sat in the rocky middle ground between ice and forest and dumped the package into her lap. She pried open the brown plastic and found slabs of pink ham where a rock-hard tortilla should've been.

When she'd thought she'd found Zeke's dead body she hadn't wanted to weep. Her body had automatically reacted. Now she wanted to cry. No one had ever done anything more thoughtful for her in her entire life. And through the years Law had done a lot for her and Zeke. This hit harder because King knew what it was to be hungry. And she knew what it was to give away a scrap of food you yearned for because someone you cared for wanted it.

She stared at the hunk of meat as though it were gold.

"Dig in. We need to get moving. If we push, we'll make it halfway by nightfall." He demolished the burrito with three bites and shrugged. "It wasn't so bad."

Khani ate with trained efficiency and kept her emotions at bay by not looking at King until again he offered her a hand. She took it without hesitation, which told her she was too far gone for anyone's good. Damn, what was she going to do with this man? He'd wormed his way past her defenses despite their world-class construction.

Like he'd said, the trail her bothers' abductors left behind made passage through the thicket bearable. Why'd she use that word? She wanted nothing bear-related in her life right now. It was bad enough her neck ached from the constant swivel she maintained.

The bushes unlocked into an airy scape sprinkled with sharp conifers and thin undergrowth. "Look." King walked to a skinny tree and noted a dangling limb snapped at the trunk. "That's deliberate." He urged her on with a hand. "So is this." A continuous pattern of step, step, scuff, corrupted the dirt.

Khani pushed ahead, taking the lead, hardly able to keep her excitement at bay. Zeke had left her a trail. He'd known she would come for him. That powered her resolve to cover as much ground as possible today. She barreled through the moss, stepped over logs, and weaved around trees. The sting in her hips didn't matter. Neither did the burn of her lungs.

One step after the other, King stayed with her.

"I guess it's later and we have some time to kill," she said, broaching the subject she'd wanted to avoid. She longed to escape it forever, but Street wouldn't let it rest much longer, and she always kept her word.

"Yeah." He gasped it out as though he never expected her to hold up to her end of the bargain.

And really, she couldn't believe it herself. "I have scars—big, small, dark, light—all over my body. My dad gave me all but three." Khani churned through the leaves and underbrush as she talked. "He wasn't a drunk. I don't think I'd have forgiven any of it if he were, but it would have been an excuse."

"There's no excuse for hurting the innocent. Not ever."

"I know that. But my mother came up with a thousand for him. He worked long hours. He had a stressful job. His boss picked on him. My grandfather had been a mean bastard."

She chuckled, but its cynicism bounced off a tree and smacked her in the face. "I don't know which of them I hated more—my mother, for her complacency, or my father. At lease he made no excuses for himself. He just liked to hit people. Especially people who weren't big enough to hit back."

Khani strangled the straps at her shoulders and pressed on. "After I was old enough to know what was going on, I know my mom had three miscarriages at his hands. I don't know how many came before. But I counted those babies lucky."

"Shit, Khani."

"Yeah." She choked on the past. Her mother's blue-bird wallpaper filled her vision. "I was washing dishes after dinner one night. My hands were covered in soap. Lord have mercy on your soul, if you missed a spot. A tea cup slipped between my fingers." She still saw the white suds fly off the rim of the ceramic as it bounced off the metal bottom of the sink. "It hit the basin and chipped. My dad threw his cup into the cabinet by my head. It splintered into a million pieces, but I didn't even jump. He'd done things like that so often..."

"You became desensitized."

"Yes."

"And that set him off."

"A little bit more every time," she agreed. "He smashed my face into the counter, told me to lick it up."

King didn't try to stop her, comfort her, and most importantly he didn't say something stupid like, 'you poor thing.' He said, "And you did."

She nodded. "I did."

They walked in silence for a long time, up a ridge and over to the next valley.

"How'd you get the other ones?"

King's voice was loud and clear, but it took her a moment to process the question. If he said anything, she'd expected more questions about her past, but she instinctively knew he meant the other ones not by her father's hand.

"Stabbed by a rebel fighter in Nigeria. Shot by a hooligan in Romania. And my happiest scar…is the skinned knee I got from crashing my bike off the ramp in Eden Park."

King held back a prickly bush with the sleeve of his jacket, allowing her to pass.

She crossed so close to him their jackets brushed. "Time for you to fess up."

"Oh yeah?"

"Yeah, you forgot to tell me what a Sherpa is?" She climbed onto a freshly fallen tree, and then hopped off the trunk, aiming for a comfy pile of leaves. The ground gave way as though it hadn't been there at all. It swallowed her like a leviathan. Her arms scrambled for ground.

Pain shot through her fingers and zinged her shoulder. A splash interrupted the burning sting in her palm. Cold enveloped her feet and calves.

She jerked to a stop. The pack fastened around her waist slipped up. It jammed into the underside of her breasts. Her hands automatically grabbed at the straps at her shoulders.

"Hang on," King gritted.

Below, a torrent of white water rushed around her legs, dragging her toward the blackness of an underground river. Panic clawed at her throat. She fought the urge to kick at the water.

Khani tilted her gaze as much as she dared to the light. A droplet of sweat slipped from King's brow and landed on her cheek. The veins in his forehead bulged. One of his legs dug into the side of the washout. Rich black soil hugged his boot. His torso spilled into the hole, while the rest of him anchored to something above. Maybe the tree trunk? Whatever it was, she hoped it would hold their combined weight.

But his arm couldn't last too much longer under the pressure.

"Can you reach your pick?" he asked.

She didn't bother answering. With her stinging hand, she reached back and groped for the axe handle. Her finger wrapped around it. She tugged. The slick end slipped through her grip. "Fuck." She tried again, this time locking her thumb around her first knuckles.

A scream threatened to escape her lips. The metal dug into her flayed flesh. She gritted past it and yanked the pick free. Blood coated the silver end. She changed hands. "Okay."

"I'm going to swing you," he panted. "When you can, drive that thing into the dirt." The pendulum started. "It won't hold long, but long enough for me to get to the rope."

The back and forth grew, the black wall growing nearer with every swing. Khani readied the axe. The wall loomed loose and unconvincing. She put her trust in King's hands—since her life was already there. She hacked into the side of the earth.

Khani dug her toes into the soggy soil. She gripped the axe with both hands. Agony lanced her left arm. Her muscles shook from the effort. She slammed the door on the pain, as she had so many times in her life. It shut out the roaring water below, the miserable death it would bring, and the aches. It no longer registered. Only her breathing blipped. In and out. In and out.

Something smacked her in the eye. Tears blurred her vision. Khani blinked furiously. The loop whipped back, and then flapped in front of her nose. She stared at it for several seconds.

The dirt gave under her right boot. Her right foot skidded down the wall. She pressed harder, finally finding purchase. The pick skidded two inches. Chunks of soil cascaded down her body.

"Grab it," King bellowed.

She swallowed. Her gaze centered the slipknot. Khani lunged for the tangle of fiber. Like a vise her right hand clamped onto the rope. All the strain of her weight and the force of her jump combined, stretching her right side.

Khani dangled in the open air. The white water rolled beneath. She turned her face away from the pit, from the past. Her chin lifted to the light, to the future. To King.

Three feet at a time he heaved her out of hell. His fingers crawled down her arms over her back to her belt. He hauled her over the moist leaves and onto his chest. She collapsed there. Her arms draped over his, laid out at his sides in surrender. Her legs splayed between his. Steam rolled off their bodies in waves. Each rapid breath rocked her.

Too soon he shifted. "Let me look at you."

Her back met the ground. It was all it took for her brain to kick-start. They didn't have time to rest. They didn't have time to snuggle on the forest floor or anywhere else.

"I'm fine." She bolted upright, using her left hand as leverage. "Son-of-a..." Khani yanked her palm from the ground only to have King yank it from her.

"The hell you are. That looks ugly." He picked a leaf from the bloody mess.

"It's just a cut." She tugged at her hand. His wrist locked around her arm and his gaze flicked to hers. "It's an ugly cut," she hedged. His bushy brow hitched so high he could catch a ride with the damn thing. "Fine," she relented. "Clean it, if you must, but make it fast."

He lifted her wrist and dragged her into his arms. His mouth was hard and more insistent than ever before. Sure he'd kissed her, but he always let her set the tempo. King's lips moved so deliberately, so insistently over hers, she forgot to demand control.

With her limbs quaking as they were, she couldn't have taken it if she'd wanted it. But the craziest thing was she didn't want it. For the first time in her life, Khani submitted to herself. She let authority slip through her fingers. Her arms relaxed. She let King take her mouth. She let him take control.

His hand firmed at her nape. He tilted her head for better access. The arm around her waist pulled her closer. The ridge of his pecs pressed against her nipples. Hot breath zipped across her lips. His tongue followed.

Khani's mouth opened at his command. His tongue coiled around hers, mating with insistent strokes and tugs. He kissed her past the pain, past sanity, to a place she'd never been before. Peace.

He levered back and stared into her eyes.

She smiled. "I suddenly have a new found appreciation for your muscles—and my desk job."

Chapter Fifteen

She hiked four miles through snow, ice, and the thatched mess of the forest with wet boots and a bloody hand. With every step she took Street loved her a little harder. His cock did too, though he seriously tried to shove those thoughts out of his mind. Khani had just opened up to him, really dropped the shield, spread her arms wide, and let the bullets fall where they may. He wasn't about to stomp all over that by trying to seduce her in a cramped tent in an even more confined sleeping bag in the middle of Alaska.

"Look at this," Khani chirped.

A narrow stream sprang seemingly from nowhere. It followed the valley they weaved through, bending and coursing with the rocky earth.

"It has to be one of the branches from the run-off."

"I want to dive in."

"Did you miss the glacial run-off part?"

Khani ground her feet into the earth and pivoted on him, her brows drawn tight. "I haven't had a shower in an entire day. My make-up is probably puddled around my chin. And I can smell myself. Right now, scrubbing off with snow sounds good. I can't feel my feet anyway." She shrugged.

"Seriously?" He cleared half the distance between them in one step.

Her hands came up. "Not seriously. I can feel them just fine. Pins and needles."

"We need to stop," he said because if he didn't she'd probably stumble her way through the pitch, sink holes, and animal traps all the way to Zeke.

"This looks like a good place for the tent." She pointed to a flat area with a row of toothpick trees on one side.

Street looked from the area to the red-cheeked woman he'd happily give his life for and blinked.

"What?" Her pack hit the ground with a thud. She rolled her shoulders in large circles and arched her neck this way and that.

"I thought I'd have to club you over the head and tie you to a tree to get you to stop."

"Remember I'm the one who does the tying." Her sinister grin flashed.

He wrapped his hand around the rope at his waist and reeled her in, the most tenacious catch of his life. "You sure about that?"

"Technicality." She walked to him, led by the rope cinched around her middle.

"I'll take it any way I can get it."

"Is that desperation I hear in your voice?"

"It wouldn't be the first time," he reminded.

"Mmm." Khani's lips clamped together. Her gaze dropped to his hands.

The knot unfastened between his fingers. As he slipped his fingers from beneath her jacket, he ran them over her thin tee and taut stomach. Her long lashes lay on her cheeks and she shuddered a breath.

"I'll get the tent set up. You have the first aid kit in your pack?" he asked.

"Yes."

"Get it out. I'm going to clean your hand better than you let me earlier, and then I'll wrap it."

"You're getting bossy, sub."

"Boss me around all you want in the bedroom and out, except for when it comes to your well-being." He settled a kiss on the tip of her nose.

"Fine. You get the tent set up and the sleeping bags out. I'll get the kit out, but before you use it I'm going to clean off."

"Don't freeze a nipple off," he chuckled.

"You laugh. If this were April, that'd be a real possibility."

"Thank goodness for summer." He winked, and then turned to their campsite. What he wouldn't give for a nice fire. This close to her brother's captors they wouldn't risk it.

Street cleared away stray branches and rocks. He tugged the roll of nylon from the bottom of his pack and wished they had a propane heater to take the chill out of the air. His nipples hardened at the thought of Khani cupping that ice-cold water onto her porcelain skin. He worked quickly, extending the poles, looping them into the arch of snaps crisscrossing the fabric.

The brownish-green dome formed in less than five. He yanked the sleeping bags from their respective packs and tossed them into the tent. On his knees, he leaned into the small space and hung his headlamp from the center hook and turned it on.

"Get out of the way," Khani's voice came high and panicked.

Street shot to his feet. His hand found the butt of his gun without thought. His eyes scanned the dimming area for a threat. He found one all right. The only threat capable of ripping his heart from his chest and stomping all over it with a smile on her face, ran toward him naked as a forest nymph.

Half of Khani's sopping hair plastered to her cheeks while the rest swung with the gate of her stride. A heap of clothes tucked beneath her arm. Hot breaths curled up from her white lips. Her pert breasts undulated. Long, creamy legs scissored, rubbing her pink folds with her furious effort to get to the tent. The strings of her boots flopped with each step. Her bare ankles stuck out of the loosened leather.

He snatched his eyeballs off the ground and yanked the door of the tent wide. "Yes, ma'am."

Khani dove headfirst, disappearing inside the shelter. "Shit."

"Shit what?" Not a thing seemed wrong from his viewpoint.

"I forgot the kit." The clack of her teeth rattling reached him.

"I think I can handle it. Get your cute arse into the sleeping bag before I forget about your hand and go to work on something else."

He used the stroll to her pack to settle himself. That was the plan at least. Funny how those things never went to form. Each stride honed his lust to the point at the tip of his dick. Street tugged a fresh pair of boxers and shirt from his pack.

"You get warm. I'll be back." He stomped toward the stream. Maybe the frigid water would check his lust. Hell, it'd probably send his balls so far inside his body he'd never find them again.

The rushing water looked inviting. And he'd had his fair share of fountain baths in the dead of

London winters. How bad could this be? He stripped in seconds and hit the deck in pushup position. Damn good thing he hadn't tested the water first. He'd have put his dirty clothes on and called it good.

He flipped to his back and scrubbed the essentials like he were on fire. His poor dick shriveled in his grasp. His nuts sucked up so high he could've spit them to the other side of the stream.

Now he knew why Khani jetted back to the tent. Street dried with his old shirt and nearly tripped over himself, tugging on his shorts, shoving his feet into his boots, and running to camp.

"No fair," Khani yelled from the interior. "I gave you a show. Where's mine."

"Trust me. There's not much to show right now." He tossed his clothes into the corner of the tent, tucked their packs into the other corner, snagged the kit from the top, and then tucked inside.

The zipper screamed closed under his hand.

"Refreshing?" Khani sat with her knees to her chest. The mummy bag cocooned her from toes to head. Only her clean face peeked out from the insulation.

The headlamp dangled between them. Its beam of light centered on his chest and then swung back to her cheek. Street steadied the light. His chill suddenly dissipated, shoved away by the realization that Khani had not an ounce of make-up on her skin. The light illuminated every fine line and every scar on her soft skin.

"You're beautiful," he breathed. Her cloudy gaze dropped. Street tucked his forefinger beneath her chin and lifted so her eyes meet his. "Beautiful." He smiled. "But I get why you wear it."

"It's my armor." The puffy bag shrugged. "We all have ours."

"What's yours?"

Street slipped his knuckles over her chin, and then cupped the side of her cheek for the briefest of seconds. "Anonymity. Humor."

"I can see that."

"Let me see your hand?"

While Khani wiggled her arm out of the sleeping bag, he shoved his legs into his then cracked the seal of the first aid kit.

"You know I can tend to my own wounds, just like you did your own." She offered him her flayed palm.

"I want to help you heal."

"Do you really think we can...help each other? Mend the scars of the past?" Her black brows scrunched.

"We'll always have scars. That's the nature of wounds, but we can minimize their appearance."

He pulled her hand into his and surveyed the raw flesh. With deliberate care, he sprayed the area with stout antibiotics, and then wrapped it with sterile gauze. Her hand cradled in his, he tangled their gazes. "Why'd you leave London?"

"I was your superior," she whispered.

"Vail is Carmen's superior and they're about to have a baby together."

Her pale lips gaped. "How'd you know?"

"She has the glow. Plus you nearly swallowed your tongue when he wanted to come along, and you gave a pretty lame excuse. I figure there was more to it. So, next excuse."

"I'm better in the field than I am behind a desk."

He set her hand in her lap and folded his arms. "You're good at anything you do, especially running away."

Both her hands balled into fists. Her growl filled the close confines. "Men make women weak, vulnerable. You get into our heads and change us from badass weapons to baby makers with tiny liabilities on our hips." She straightened her hands as though she were flinging him off and all his complicated stickiness.

"Did you ever think that they chose that life? That that's what they want?"

She barked a laugh and ground her fist against her forehead. "That's the worst part of it all. They choose to be weakened."

"Weakened in one way. Strengthened in others." He shrugged. "Was I the first person you ever had sex with?" He didn't think so, but the way she acted he must have broken some treaty she had with herself.

"No." Her hands dropped to her lap. "But you were the first to make me break my rule." He waited for it. "Never have sex with someone you're going to see again."

"No repeats?" He gawked.

"No."

"No matter how good."

"They usually aren't that good."

"Why me?"

"We haven't repeated."

"Not yet," he said.

"Because you make me weak." Her gaze lasered into the top of the tent. She blinked furiously.

Street grabbed her injured hand and brought it to his mouth. He kissed the tips of her fingers, the ball of her palm. When he raised his gaze she lowered hers. "Choosing vulnerability is the greatest show of strength."

"Or stupidity," she amended.

"Love is bold."

"What do you know about love?" She spat the words, but not in rage. Real bafflement clouded her eye, hitched her jaw.

"Not much," he said honestly. It's not like his life had been a prime example for the concept. In fact his had been the opposite.

"Well," she huffed. "I know enough to tell you love is fictitious."

"Yeah? Tell that to your brother. You've crossed thousands of miles and are ready to take on the Russian mob all to protect him."

"That's different."

"That's love. Familial or otherwise. Boundless. Inexplicable. It makes you fucking mad and elated at the same time." He tugged her mouth a hair's breadth from his. "It makes you do things you never thought you'd do."

Her granite gaze roved his face. "Like?"

"Submitting." He whispered the word over her mouth. "I'm yours, Khani. Do with me what you will." Amazingly, the frigid water's effects had worn off. He gulped and then begged. "Just please, do something to me."

Chapter Sixteen

His lids fluttered shut. The behemoth of a man with his broad shoulders and hands strong enough to crush her skull without trying had relinquished control...to her. More surprising than his submission was that with him—now—she didn't need it. The panic she'd always fought in the minutes before her lovers were secured had been replaced by carnal need. It licked her clit like a heavy tongue, steady and insistent.

Usually the desire came after she'd established her dominance, after they were subjugated. Only then did she relax enough to let her body take over. Only then did she unleash her longing.

For too long she'd imprisoned herself, denied herself out of fear.

"Your surrender means more than anything. Your surrender...allows my own." Khani gathered the material around her shoulders and levered onto her knees. She leaned over King, but for a wholly different reason than she'd have before.

"I'll never be able to thank you enough for that." Her lips met his in tender pecks. One by one, she trailed them down his hardy jaw. His stubble prickled her skin. She dragged her mouth across his to the other side and loved him in a line to his ear. Khani pressed her cheek against his. "But I'm sure going to try."

A soft moan rumbled in his throat.

"You want me to try?" She teased.

"Yes."

His breath tickled the hollow of her clavicle. She pulled the collar of his T-shirt wide, sank her teeth into the base of his neck, and sucked. King's hips jerked, brushing his thighs against hers through the layers of their sleeping bags. Her tongue raked his skin. Salt and sex. She drank him like a tequila shot. Her mouth popped off his flesh leaving behind a red stain on his skin.

She slid her fingers over the angry mark. Never before had she scored a lover. Not with a crop. Not with a whip. Not even with her nails. "I'm sorry. I don't know—"

"Don't apologize." He turned his head to face her and opened his eyes. The mix of green and brown calmed her on sight. "If it leaves a scar, it'll be my happiest one."

Her hand slipped around his nape. She pulled him close and smashed their lips together. His hands stayed by his side, but his mouth and tongue participated fully, giving as much as they received. Her entire body played into the kiss. The lips of her sex rubbed in maddening time with the roll of her hips.

Mews and pants seeped out between their mouths. Desperation tightened her throat, cutting off her flow of oxygen. Khani broke the kiss. She shoved the suffocating fabric around the gentle curve of her square hips, and then reached for King's hands.

"Touch me." The roughened skin of his fingers and palms scratched her sensitive flesh. The tips of her breast stabbed into his hands in return.

Khani dropped her hands from around his and he held perfectly still. His reddened bottom lip hung. "Are you sure?"

"No one ever has. I want you to."

"Never?"

"You with your mouth, but other than that, no."

"Fuck me," he sighed.

"We'll get there."

His Adam's apple flipped a cartwheel in his throat. "Yes." He touched tentatively at first, no more than a whisper over her skin.

She blamed his mouth for this adventure. Before, with him, she climaxed so quickly. All it had taken was few thrusts of his heavy cock and a tug of her nipple and she careened over the edge of control, unable to halt the inevitable and aggressive release.

He tweaked her right bud. Her back bowed. She clutched his shoulder with her injured hand. Pleasure masked the pain. King cupped her mounds. A hot breeze wafted over her swollen tips, amplifying the thrill that rolled through her limbs.

"Please," he pleaded, his mouth hovering over her crimson nipples.

"Yes," she nearly begged in return.

King opened his mouth wide and shoved half of her left breast inside his mouth. His fingers molded the other, which seemed to double in size from the excess blood flow and attention he lavished onto them. She anchored herself to his powerful shoulders, hating the shirt that stood between her skin and his skin.

A flick of his tongue turned her attention. "Yes." She arched into his mouth and the snap of his wet tongue became more insistent. Her clit pulsed, begging for attention. Khani sucked a lung-full of air, and then another, but failed to tame her desire.

Pressure mounted on her right nipple. King's lips pinched the peak between his lips and pulled slowly off. His chest heaved. He gulped air as greedily as she, which meant he lusted as powerfully as she. That tidbit ratcheted her urgency.

"Khani, has anyone touched your silky pink lips," he drew a breath, "or your swollen little clit?"

Her throat clogged. How could she answer? Yes. No. They were both true. No. No one she'd ever allowed to touch her, no one she'd ever wanted to touch her so intimately had. Yes. Someone had broken her will in half, had shattered her to prove an ugly point.

"The night before I took Zeke and left, I wore a short shirt out with friends. When I got home my father slammed me into the counter, ripped my panties off, and beat me until my clit bled."

"Is your father alive?"

She shook her head, unsure whether she could pronounce a single word with the mishmash of emotions burdening her tonsils.

King went palms up. "Hey, you're here with me. I'm here for you, to do anything and everything that will make you feel good. That's off limits. Okay." He shrugged. "There are a thousand other ways I can pleasure you."

"I want you to." She placed her palms against his. "I've never wanted anyone to, but I want to feel your fingers slide between my flesh."

"What about my lips?"

"Hell yes," she choked.

"My tongue?"

Her knees buckled, but she caught herself against his hands. "Yes."

"Say my name," he ordered.

"Don't I give the orders around here?" She smiled and used her shoulder to wipe a stray tear from her cheek.

"Say my name, Khani." He dragged her hands to his face and framed them around his square jaw. "Tell me you know who's here with you..." The outside of his knuckles skimmed over her cheek, across her breasts, and then grazed her belly. "...who's loving you with his hands..." His head dipped between her breasts. Her hands stayed with him as he licked the underside of her aching breast. "...with his mouth..." King placed a kiss over her heart. His hands anchored on either side of her hips. He leaned back and tangled their gazes. "....with everything I possess."

"King." Khani's heart squeezed, suddenly too large to fit inside her chest cavity.

His smile lit the dark confines of the tent. "That's right." He kissed the tips of her middle fingers, and then lowered them to her sides. He tugged the shirt over his head and tossed it away. The pink scar on his shoulder zinged lusty memories to her already aching core. The gnarled skin from a bullet that hit too close to home didn't have quite the effect.

King ditched his sleeping bag and boxers as though it weren't so close to freezing just outside their shelter. Inside, however, they'd worked up quite a sultry heat. He flipped onto his belly with his legs stretching the edge of the tent opposite her. The rounds of his shoulders ripped with his engaged muscles. His head drifted from her nipples, grazing like a wild beast over her belly.

Her breath hitched, and then quaked her lungs.

"I've got you, troop." His hand stayed planted on the ground, but his mouth planted elsewhere.

"Oh, God," she gasped.

He eased his lips from her slick sex. "Oh, King," he corrected. "Blow me over, you wax?"

"I don't like hair down there," defending her choice.

"Your brother might have to save himself. I don't think I'm leaving this spot...ever." He slid a finger over her tender nub.

Hell, she might never let him leave.

King tilted his head, flattened his tongue, and slipped it from the cleft of her ass, across her wet channel, to the very tip of her clit. He pulled his tongue into his mouth. His eyes clamped shut and he groaned like a grizzly. Her breasts bounded from her frantic breaths. The tips glistened in the beam of light.

He came back for more, swiping desperately over her pulsing bundle of nerves. Khani knotted her hands in her hair to keep from gripping his. She didn't want to impede his rhythm in any way. Already she hovered, her insides threatening to rocket away and leave her body behind. Her breaths turned to moans. They crept higher toward keens.

His tongue froze on the tip of her clit. Khani's hips rocked against the slick tip. He retreated an inch. "Not yet." His head shook. "I'm just getting started."

"I won't last long."

"Good thing there's no cap on the number of orgasms I plan to give you."

Wetness coated his mouth. His head hovered inches from the junction of her thighs. A deep groove ran the length of his spine, hard earned muscles forming a trench. Banded brawn wrapped the slopes of his naked ass. The sight assaulted her restraint.

"King," she said.

When he raised his eyes all the things she wanted to say stayed glued to her tongue. *I think I love you. You're the most amazing man I've ever met. If I wake tomorrow and you're gone, I'll treasure you forever and the gifts you've given me.* She settled for, "Thank you."

"Don't thank me yet." His chuckle vibrated her lips. He speared his tongue and lashed her clit, grinding his mouth against the whole of her sex.

Sharp pain tingled her scalp and she realized her grip threatened to yank the hair from her head. "Yes, King. Please, yes." She pumped against him.

The orgasm swamped her. Every muscle in her honed body quivered with pure delight. Her head tossed back and her toes pointed toward the sky.

Mother fucking tears collected in her eyes, turning her into the vulnerable, weeping sap she'd always feared a man would transform her into. And at the same time she felt stronger than she ever had. Blasting bad guys in the head, throwing herself into the middle of a firefight, or dancing with blades, none of it compared to the bravery it took for her to face down her greatest fear and come through the other side whole.

Still she felt the immediate need to re-establish herself. "On your ass, King. Hands by your side."

"Yes, troop." His tongue skated across his lips, licking her cream into his mouth. Slowly, deliberately showing off the body that made her forget herself, he sat and leaned back on both hands. The lines of his abdomen contracted, punctuating the sleekness of his hefty build. The notch of steel corded at his hips, made the perfect handle for her leg to cling to.

The tears receded, overrun by carnal lust. "Yes, indeed." Her orgasm coated the inside of her thighs. She shoved the sleeping bag over her knees and wiggled out of its confines, abrading her intimate flesh in the process. It rekindled a fire that never banked...and likely never would.

Pre-cum beaded at the slit of his plump crown. She placed her index finger atop the clear liquid and speared it over the smoothness of his head. As she had before, she licked the excess from the pad of her finger. Her mouth watered. The need to choke him deep had her humming, but the unabated throb between deep inside her cunt commanded attention.

Khani straddled his lap as she had too damn long ago. This time things were so very different. King wasn't restrained and neither was she. She wrapped her arms around his neck—like she'd wanted to do before.

His steady gaze centered hers. One torturous inch at a time, Khani lowered herself onto his cock. The pressure of his broad width compounded. She sank lower, enjoying the swell of his head as it bombarded her body. Knees spread wide, she exhaled and invited him farther inside. The map work of veins strapping his dick worked like a ribbed dildo, strumming her from the core out.

"Put your hands on me," she ordered.

As though he'd been waiting for the words, as though he'd known they were coming, his hands molded against her lower back and worked them up. The move pulled her impossibly closer. Their noses brushed. Their breaths mingled. Their gazes wed. She seated him fully and they stilled there, unmoving, for a heap of heartbeats.

Then his hands moved. Those big fingers sank into her bottom. She lifted off him to the tip, and then plunged hard. Her gasp ricocheted off the fabric and collided with his bark of pleasure. Again she pounded their bodies together. And again. Each time King's arms powered the effort a little more, until soon they shared the responsibility of their pleasure.

She'd never shared any part of the duty. She'd never trusted a person enough to want to try. Not until King.

Khani hugged him impossibly close with her arms, with her core.

He shouted a curse that rang like music in her ears. His deft hands tilted her hips, opening them and her clit to the firm ridge of his pelvis.

Pleasure rippled through her. Her hold doubled. Her breaths grew shallow. "Fuck me. Fuck me."

"I'm loving you," he strangled. "I'm loving you." His jaw clenched another curse. "Are you still on birth control?"

"Yes," she moaned as much in overwhelming bliss as in answer. "Come with me, King. Come."

His head arched to the unseen stars. He did as she demanded, pulsing his heated orgasm into her womb. Another first. One that—as much as it terrified her—compounded her release.

Her heart stampeded through her chest as though it might crash right through her chest. King tucked his head against her roaring heart and panted. Sweat slicked their bodies, sealing them together.

For how long? Khani didn't know, but she hoped for a longer time than she'd ever imagined sharing with another human being...even Zeke.

King collapsed back onto his yawning sleeping bag, tugging her with him, seemingly as content to maintain the bond they formed. He pulled her sleeping bag over their bodies and held her atop his chest.

Chapter Seventeen

An alarm trilled through his dream, shattering the glass walls. Shards rained around him, pinging off the ground and bouncing back toward his face. Street's eyes popped open at the same time as Khani's murky greys. For a stunned second they stared at one another.

Touch by exquisite touch the dream—his reality—dripped back into his conscious mind.

Khani buried her face under his neck. Even when she'd been vulnerable she'd never been embarrassed. "What is it?" he whispered.

"I don't want to get up. I don't want to leave this tent. I don't want to face the day." Her arms coiled around him. "Because now I have something else I don't want to lose."

"I'm not going anywhere, except down on you and inside of you the next chance I get. The only way I'm leaving is if you make me."

She smiled, but it held more than a hint of sadness. "I might make you." Her head shook. "I'm not good at relationships. I've never been in one and I'm not sure I won't fuck it up."

"And I'm sure no matter how much you push me away, I'll always belong to you."

Khani crawled up his body and laid one on him. He starched at first contact. Too soon she rolled off him. Her grin beamed in the dim room. "Saddle up, cowboy."

"Is that a euphemism for...you want to bone again?"

She giggled. "No. It's American for get ready, we've gotta go."

"Damn." He winked and groped for his pack, ready to pull on some clothes now that the sleeping bag and her sweet warmth didn't drape his body. "How about we steer clear of washouts today?"

"And bears," she said through the knit of her sweater. Mussed black hair sprang from the head hole. "And wolves."

"Wolves? Who cares about them? They're like large dogs."

She popped out of the top of the sweater, her eyebrows cranked high. "You obviously didn't see *The Grey*."

A full-out belly laugh cramped his sides.

"Oh, when we get back we're watching it." Her nose scrunched. "I'm making *you* watch it. I have no desire to see it again. Especially after this trip."

"I take it it's less *Dances with Wolves* and more *Cujo*?"

"Um, yeah." Her hair bobbed.

"So, we're going after bad guys with guns, but avoiding cute teddy bear and fluffy pups." He tugged his shirt over his head, hiding his head as she rolled her eyes. "Got it."

"I'm going to get it," she threatened.

"Promise?"

"Hell yes, but not right now." She shoved her socked feet into her boots and opened the tent's zipper. "I'll see you outside in two. I have to pee."

He couldn't wipe the stupid grin off his mouth. Khani rolled her eyes and groaned for effect, and then crawled out of their hideaway. Street finished dressing, packed their bags, rolled the shelter, and stuffed it into his ruck by the time she returned.

Khani plopped onto the ground in front of him and laced her boots. "Why the smirk?"

"You're kidding me right?" He swung the pack onto his shoulders. "I've been dreaming about getting my hands on you for more than a year."

Smile lines bracketed her mouth. "This is crazy."

"What exactly."

Her lips pursed. "My brother's being tortured, if he's not already dead, and I'm here making googley eyes at you."

"On your way to save him. Stop guilting yourself."

She recoiled as though he'd ripped one. "Easy for you to say. No one's ever been dependent on you for every little thing. We left home when Z was twelve, but for as long as I can remember I'm the only one who made sure he was fed, bathed, and got enough sleep every night. If I didn't fix us something to eat, we didn't eat."

"He's a grown man, troop. You did a job you shouldn't have had to do. You did it well. But you don't have to shoulder him anymore."

"Oh," she tossed her hands. "So, I should just leave him in the hands of the Russian mob?"

"That's not what I said and you know it." Street hefted her pack. He crossed to her. Leaves and small sticks crackled under his boots. He extended his hand as a peace offering. "Don't pick a fight with me because you're feeling exposed. Last night was the best night of my life. It's okay if you feel the same. It's okay if you don't. I don't expect you to drop your weapons and birth our very own liability."

Khani's cool fingers wrapped around his hand. She stood without much help from him. "When I don't know what to do with myself I get prickly. Bitchy." She stared off several seconds before meeting his gaze again. "You deserve better than me."

He smoothed a kiss over her dry lips. "We deserve each other." King believed that with his whole heart. He'd never been able to share himself with anyone. Khani shared a similar background. They'd both developed ways to cope with the insanity. Their unique survival mechanisms complimented one another. If only he could get her to see that.

She didn't respond to his comment. Her hand slipped from his and onto her ruck. "I need to run. You up for it?"

"I've been chasing your tail for thousands of miles. What's four more—uphill—with fifty pounds on my back?" His gaze double checked their heading on his watched. "After you, my lady."

Pounding up the side of the mountain they no longer needed the rope tethered between them. Every strike of their boots met with solid rock the color of Khani's eyes. The trees—their cover—thinned, leaving them both exposed. Street found himself feeling prickly.

They fell into a rhythm they'd found last night. The balls of their boots marched higher and higher, but their pace remained even. Purpose propelled them. Pine flavored the thin air. Sweat added another layer to the bouquet.

A snap to their right stopped them both mid-stride. Street crouched. Khani drew her weapon. Their chests fluctuated, but not a sound whispered through their lips. Another crack echoed through the green ferns and needles. Not a gun shot. Those popped more than cracked. This sounded as though a giant pared limbs from a tree to make his toothpick.

Street's gaze pivoted across the slanted ground. Khani's lids gaped as wide as headlights, searching for the threat. They were still a mile from the cabin. This was a little far out to have a lookout, but stranger things had happened. He should've thought about that sooner. He'd been about to call time on her sprinted run. No way would he barrel into the unknown without a plan.

"There," Khani barely breathed.

He followed her gaze fifty yards down the mountain. The green top of an aspen rocked slowly. The sight was nothing unusual of the side of a windy slope, except when he looked at all the trees around it. They stood soldier straight in the still air.

The hairs on his nape prickled. Only one thing was big enough to move a tree that large and he didn't want to meet it.

"Run." If it were possible, he hollered the whisper.

His nerves took off before he did, careening dangerously over his veins. Khani stood, her feet seemingly solidified into the side of the earth. He'd never thought fear capable of paralyzing her, but the evidence blocking their escape proved him wrong.

"We're not supposed to run." She whispered the words while keeping her gaze trained on the spot in the distance.

"Then walk, quickly," he prodded.

The hand straining the metal of her pistol shook. "We're supposed to confront it. Stand our ground."

"Piss the ground more like. It's far enough away we can exit the stage with no one the wiser." He put his hands on her shoulder and hip and nudged her forward.

"Don't move." She commanded.

His daft body complied. He held perfectly still.

"He's coming to say, 'Hi.'" Khani squeaked.

Street slid his gaze to the side and saw a wall of brown charging. How the mother-fuck had he cleared the distance that fast?

"Stand beside me, make yourself as big as possible, don't hold his gaze, and don't move."

Every instinct inside Street's body roared to life. Every one of them told him to run. His training told him to grab his gun and aim between the two amber eyes boring down on him. Khani told him to hold his ground.

Dumb as it might be, he listened to her. He stood to every millimeter of his six feet six inches. He spread his convulsing chest like a roided-up gym-rat. He took one step forward, placing himself a foot in front of Khani. He dropped his gaze to the ground. Each ferocious scrape of the grizzly's massive paws and blade-sharp claws mauled the earth. And he prayed Khani's firing hand steadied.

The rock shook beneath his feet. The air crackled with tension. The bear closed in on them. Fifteen yards. Stride. Ten. Stride.

Street's muscles contracted, bracing for certain impact. A blow sure enough to shatter every bone in his body.

The beast slammed on the breaks. Its front feet skidded on the slate. Shoulders as wide as Street's torso rolled, pressing into the rock. The bear's snout flared, black and shining in the morning light. It huffed their scent. Rows and fucking rows of pointed teeth stood on display ten feet away. A clamor blatant and guttural erupted from its cavernous mouth.

"You don't want to eat us, do you?" Khani spoke in an even tone, stunning the shit out of him, the shit that hadn't already incinerated inside his gut. "You just want us out of your territory and we're happy to go, just walk away."

Five-inch razor blades attached to its paws gouged the ground. Rocks broke from the ground and flew. They skittered to the side, pinging down the grade.

"Don't make me shoot you, bear. It'll alert Zeke's captors and give away our position."

"Will a shot kill it or just make it angry...er?"

"One way to know. What's it gonna be, bear?" Khani asked in the same droll tone.

"If we lose the element of surprise, they'll kill Zeke before we get there."

"I know," she said with a hint of agitation.

The bear responded with another scallop of the ground.

He had no desire to kill the bear. It was brutish and majestic. At the same time he'd choose himself over the animal any day of the week, and he'd choose Khani ten times on Sunday.

Street lifted his gaze, centering his cross hairs on the grizzly's yellow one. The creature's eyes conveyed intelligence, even more than some people possessed. It pinned its ears back and chuffed a warning. Street filled his lungs. The pungent odor of free-range fur burned his nostrils.

As a kid, he'd learned to center a dart from the far side of Bryan's Pub. He'd made the old man a ton of money. Unwitting patrons bet against Street every time. Every time they'd choke up their change to Bryan. In turn the bloke fed him dinner most nights of the week.

Street yanked his ice pick from his ruck with his left hand. With his right he jerked his fixed blade from the scabbard on his thigh. He unleashed the oxygen he held in a bellow that stripped the lining from his throat.

He jacked the axe high. On a lunge he hurled it. The handle scraped the tips of his fingers, and then sailed through the air. It sank into the bear's mussy pelt. The skin on its shoulder peeled open.

The bear shied. Sunlight filtered through the trees glinting off the visible point of the double picked steel. The other sharp end sank deep inside the beast's shoulder.

Street filled his lungs. He shouted and lunged again, his knife ready.

Those massive claws shuffled, conceding two steps. Then another. The mammoth's head reared. Its long snout bit at its injured shoulder.

Street lifted his arms, making himself larger. He snarled and ate the space the grizzly relinquished. Now that the bear walked away from him—now that pictures of mauled flesh didn't corrupt his brain—he noticed the animal's back only reached his belly button. The imposing creature was young, maybe a few years old. If it had been a full-grown bear they would've been fucked.

He followed the grizzly's lazy retreat a football field or more down the grade. Slowly he allowed the gap to grow between them. Thirty yards away the brute leaned its injured side into a tree and scraped its shoulder across the bark. Street's axe clanked to the ground. The beast lumbered off toward the creek where he and Khani had cleaned up the previous night.

Damn. If they'd run into that thing without weapons... He shook his head and watched the animal until it was little more than a speck on the horizon. Feeling certain they could continue on without worrying about that particular bear sniffing up their asses again, Street turn and headed back toward where he'd left Khani.

The things he knew about grizzly bears fit in half the scabbard where he placed his knife, but he knew predators. Most adhered to the one per territory rule. He hoped it was the same for bears. Adrenaline zapped, the climb took longer than it had the first time.

Sweat soaked his under-layer. A U-shape darkened the forearm of his sleeve where he'd swiped the perspiration from his brow. Luckily, the sun burned brightly and the temperature had risen into the forties, which meant he wouldn't die of hypothermia.

He used narrow trees to hoist himself up the slope. They needed a break for food, dry clothes, and a plan. His yell had been loud enough to travel the mile to the place where the Russians held Zeke, if they'd been listening. But the sound had been so savage it's likely they would've believed it came from an animal.

Four individual claw marks dredged into the rock inches from where he and Khani had been standing. A foot closer the second gash marred the earth. Street shook his head, and then lifted his gaze to find his woman. She'd marked him last night. It seemed only fair that he claimed her as well. Only his woman wasn't in the place where he'd left her.

His eyes slanted left and then right. No black hair. No black leather boots. No Khani.

Street's tongue swelled, but he managed to swallow past it. She probably had to pee. After that encounter he was surprised there weren't two puddles on the ground in front of him.

One step at a time, he turned in a slow circle, waiting for her to pop from behind a tree and blast him for not following her directives where the bear was concerned. The longer he waited the tighter the constriction of his throat banded.

Was there another bear, one that had come from behind them? His head shook before the question fully formed in his mind. No. He'd have heard her shots. Plus there was no blood and no mutilated body. His stomach pitched at the image his brain created.

None of the tree limbs hung; none were snapped at awkward angles. Except for the spot where the grizzly had been and the line of their defense, the ankle-high plants stood perky and green. She hadn't struggled with anyone or anything.

Had she left him? Again his head shook. No, she wouldn't have gone ahead without him unless... she found out about his digging into their backgrounds or... Or what? He didn't know.

Agitation propelled him forward. His gaze roved for any sign of her, any clue as to what had happened to her. Street followed the route they'd plotted yesterday toward the cabin. His heart scaled the craggy walls of his chest.

A syrupy cloud drifted in, blanketing the sunshine. It thickened the air. Each breath he heaved required extra effort. He gave it. He gave it all, churning his heavy legs up the rising slope in a sprint.

Fifty feet of push and constant swivel produced nothing. No Khani. No direction in which to proceed. His teeth gritted. The joints of his knuckles threatened to pop. Busting his arse earlier had revealed the abductors' trail. Out of options, Street hit the deck, palms and cheek to the ground.

The rocky earth held its secrets, refusing to reveal an obvious path. He smashed the meaty side of his fist against the ungiving rock. His head tilted and he choked back a growl that burned his raw throat. A stone's throw away clean brass against the grey expanse caught his eye.

Street lurched at the blip. He pinched a bullet between his thumb and forefinger. The inscription on the end of the brass read Winchester 45 Auto. The full metal jacket matched Khani's ammo to the T. He squeezed the cool metal in the center of his palm. Either she left him a clue or she dropped one in a frantic effort to reload. Again, if the later were true, he'd have heard the shots.

He jumped to his feet and bolted up the route with silent steps. Ears opened, he tuned out the hum of bugs, the random caws of a hawk looking to get laid, the thump of his heart. Nothing. Yet.

Several yards ahead another bullet lay between the cracks of the rock. Street pocketed both bullets and pushed on. Hope solidified his rapid strides.

"`Suka." A deep rumbling voice spat the word. It echoed through the stolid pines, but not at him. The curse was too faint to be meant for him. And he was many foul words, but he was no man's bitch.

Neither was Khani.

Street planted himself behind the widest tree in the vicinity and searched the horizon for movement. He pressed forward two hundred yards, dodging between pines not bigger around than his thigh.

Thirty feet away two beefy men held each of her elbows. She twisted and bucked, but gave no real effort to escape. They dragged her toward the narrow porch of a hickory log cabin about the size of a double-car garage. European cars, not American. The west building looked more like an outhouse than a shed. A length of chain and a padlock secured the door to the small but hearty structure.

Zeke was still alive. A dead prisoner didn't require lock and key. Relief loosened the flow of his breaths. Khani would've seen the silver metal and drawn the same conclusion.

"Please," Khani sobbed, "let me go. I don't know who you are. What do you want with me?"

"Shut up." The son-of-a-bitch on her right jerked her arm. His reedy voice held a thick Russian bur. "You stick your nose where it doesn't belong, you get it cut off."

Khani belted a shriek scripted for a Hollywood drama. The sound was so stratified with fear, he had to remind himself she was putting on a show.

Street extricated his phone and sent the coordinates and time for the HELO extraction. It'd take them every bit of an hour to get here from Anchorage. He just hoped they didn't need it sooner.

The front door of the cabin flew open. It banged against the weathered logs and swung back toward the frame. A fat hand short a pinkie slammed against the door, stopping it cold. The stocky man pounded his way onto the stoop. Craters scared his wide face. A scowl added to the revoke of his presence.

"˘Tchyo za ga˘lima?" The apparent leader tossed his whole arm into the air. "That's not a grizzly bear."

"We found her in the woods less than a mile away, Iosif." The taller of the two explained with a hitch of his thumb down the mountain.

"Why bring her here?" The leader barked.

"We don't know what she was doing out there. Maybe she nose around and find—"

"Zatk˘nis." Iosif's hand sliced the air. "Take her back where you found her and let her go."

"But—" One of the men protested, but the sentence was severed by another stroke of the man's hand.

The leader's mouth opened to speak, but then closed. He leaned into the cabin, as though someone required his attention. He spoke, but Street couldn't make out what he said. His Russian wasn't that good. Someone else in the cabin made the count at least four to two.

Good odds.

Iosif's wide shoulders shrugged. His gaze swiveled to Khani. Black eyes narrow. He really looked at her for the first time since he'd stomped onto the porch. A rye smirk curled one side of his mouth. "She is," he called into the foggy interior. His ugly laugh curdled the contents of Street's stomach. "Bring her to me. Grisha needs some fun after all his hard work."

Street drew his S & W. He centered the chuckling man's pock-marked forehead and braced his trigger finger on the guard.

Come on, troop. Make your move, I've got you.

He willed her to thrash the mothers, to give him a sign she was ready to end this charade. But she didn't know he covered her pert ass. The muscles in his forearms quaked. His grip tested the metal's strength. A string of curses ticked across his brain.

The goons ushered her forward.

Khani barred her legs on the bottom step. "No. Please. Let me—"

The douche with brutish muscles and a Mickey Mouse voice kicked the tip of his boot at the back of her knee. They shoved her at the other man.

Iosif's arms locked around Khani's waist. He snuggled her to his chest and buried his head at the side of her neck. Street tossed his inner hooligan behind bars. These guys would get theirs soon enough. Let them think they had the upper hand.

"And the bear?" The man lifted his mouth from her neck, licked his lips, and eyed the two subordinates.

"We chased it off," the biggest chump said.

The hell they had.

"Couldn't have it eat Slaughter. Not before we are ready," Mickey added.

Chump smacked him on the back of the head, and then they both looked at Khani.

"Don't worry." Iosif smiled, revealing an incisor as incomplete as his pinkie. "If she stays to play, we have plenty of time to convince her not to talk. If she doesn't play, she won't talk again." He winked at Khani, who didn't see the gesture.

She tucked her head against the man's chest. Her muffled cries bled their way to Street's ears. The volume shied hysterics, but only by a degree or two. He kept reminding himself she wasn't a crier, that this was all a spectacle. Still, the more she bawled the harder he drove his shoulder into the tree to keep from barreling into the fray.

Scar-pinkie held Khani close and pulled her inside the cabin. He grabbed the edge of the door to close it.

"What about us?" Mickey squeaked.

"Maybe after we're done you can have a turn." The man's pink tongue peeked through the gap in his teeth, and then it lolled out of his mouth, licking his chops. "You go see if you can work some information out of our other guest, but whatever you do, don't kill him. Dead men don't talk."

"Oh God," Khani wailed. Such a pitiful sound streaming from a woman would cause any normal human being distress. The mobster's grin widened. The door closed slowly, sealing his woman inside with at least two brutal men.

Chapter Eighteen

The stench of Iosif's pits and cigar-smoke burned her eyes. Heat radiated from a wood-burning oven in the corner, compounding the fetor. The handle of the man's sheathed blade ground into her ribs. His fingers dug into her back.

"You want her mouth or her cunt?" the sick son-of-a-bitch asked.

Playing victim, even for the purpose of breaching the tiny contingent of corrupt Russians, irritated her more than the smell. She'd have preferred to kick the door in, guns drawn, with King at her back.

This was what she got for staring after him like a love-struck dummy. He'd challenged a grizzly to save her. At the very least he deserved her awe. And she'd given it, gawking after his sexy ass as he herded a beast four times his size down the side of a mountain.

Her back had been exposed, which nearly cost her life. Their shouted, "Ey," had been the only warning she had to their presence. The guy she dubbed Soprano aimed a rifle at her chest and yelled in his native tongue. It took effort not to laugh. His vehemence that he should shoot her and leave her for the bear severely diminished exertion it took to hold back her chuckle. Instead she exchanged it for newly-discovered impulse control. She managed to *not* drop to the ground and draw on him.

A fraction of a second before she planned to reach for the WC at her side his friend cleared the line of trees with his shiny pistol at the ready. Cue hysterics. She was a graduate student—cough, cough—researching the ghymbo limbus ferns that only sprouted in spring along this segment of this ice field in all the world. Her graduation relied on it. She wasn't hunting, but if they were, a bear was just heading down the hill.

They'd been skeptical and probably hadn't understood half of what she'd said, but the bead the new addition held on her chest dropped to the forest floor she kept gesturing toward. She'd turned away pointing across the slope about the bear and used the opportunity to slip the 1911 and holster from her belt and slip it inside an outer pocket of her ruck.

Of course, shuffling through her pocket had drawn their attention and their eager hands. The heavy, as she called him, hurried forward, rattling on in Russian.

"I don't understand." She had shrugged, yanked the map from her pocket, and thrust it at him, discreetly zipping the thing closed behind her.

He'd crumpled the map under his boot and clamped her wrists behind her back. And here she was in the place she'd longed to be for the last four days. Only she didn't have her backup. A chuckle resounded in her brain. Two days ago she'd scoffed at his involvement. Today she relied on him. She'd bet her life King had found the cabin before she'd been sequestered inside. But she couldn't bet Zeke's.

As much as she wanted to make this last, to hear them beg for mercy as they surely would, she didn't have the luxury.

With her head against the asshole's chest, she surreptitiously eyed the interior. The main room was no bigger than a low rent flat in London; a one-serve kitchenette and mini fridge added to the effect. An open doorway gave view to another room. A bed with a hideous maroon and hunter-green comforter had been wedged in the corner probably fifty years ago when the cabin had been built with thought to function and none to feel.

The smoke curled up from a cigar on a coffee table. The cramped living area boasted a threadbare love seat and wingback chair. A man nearly as big as King reclined on the sofa, causing the center of it to sag. He held another cigar between his lips.

"You take the end with teeth." He puffed a stream of grey like an industrial park. "I'll take her ass." Tattoos peeked out from the collar and cuffs of his oxford. She wanted to strangle him with the blue cloth. Who the hell wore a dress shirt on an Alaskan ice field?

Someone who didn't get their hands dirty. Her gaze dropped to his hands. Not a bruise marred his knuckles. Not a hangnail ruffled his shining manicure.

Iosif's hand plowed into her hair. Pain registered a second before he jerked her head back. His near black gaze danced over her. "Ooohhh, look at her face." He turned her head to the other man. "She must like it rough."

Her sobs died. "Yes, she does," Khani purred.

The man thrust her to arm's length. His eyes considered her more closely.

She winked at him. His mouth opened to speak. She placed her finger over his lips.

"And she likes to do the penetrating." Khani yanked the knife from his belt. With a force developed over years of hand-to-hand combat and lifting, she rammed the blade into his carotid.

One of Iosif's hands wrapped around hers. His nails sunk into her jacket. A gurgle erupted from his throat, bringing a river of crimson with it. Oops. She must have severed his esophagus too.

He lunged at her as though he could do anything but slowly die.

Khani's gaze lifted in time to see the glint of the pistol the man on the couch pulled from the cushion.

Her grip on the knife firmed. She positioned Iosif's draining body in front of hers and hoped his thick muscles would stop the bullets whizzing at her in rapid-fire succession. *Boom. Boom. Boom. Boom.*

Iosif jerked with the first four shots. After that only the impetus of the bullet's impact moved the body she hefted as a shield. Too damn bad the corpse didn't have a gun on him. Hers hid in the pack, clinging laboriously to her back.

Her back.

If the other two came running she'd have a mess on her hands. She kept one quarter of her attention trained on the door. Holding the hundred-plus kilo man took most of her concentration. That and counting the number of shots that pelted into her human armor.

Click. Click. Finally he'd run out of bullets. For how long she didn't know. Khani dropped Iosif's weight, but kept hold of the knife.

"Grisha?" she yelled at the man scrambling to his feet with the useless pistol in hand. His startled gaze met hers. Then his hands clambered toward the back of his belt.

Taking a play from King's book, she launched the bloody blade through the air. It sank into the left side of the man's expansive chest.

He straightened, and then hunched. His hands gripped the blade and yanked it free. He bellowed like an animal. She thought for certain she'd be dodging its point, but he dropped it to the ground. The metal clattered on the pier and beam floor.

Khani dove for the pocket. She wrestled blindly with the zipper, keeping her eyes on Grisha. Even wounded he could kill her with his bare hands. She could kill him with hers, but why chance it. Zeke needed her whole to get him out of here.

His good arm fished under his shirt.

The unforgiving barrel of her Wilson Combat met her fingers. She palmed it and righted the gun in her grip as she stood.

The familiar *ting* of a pin leaving the home of its grenade pulled her attention upright. Grisha yanked the small round explosive from a chain around his neck.

Fuck.

Chapter Nineteen

Mickey and company shoved their way into the tiny shed, hollering and cursing like they had something to say. Street left his pack behind a tree. He stole from cover with his S & W on his hip and his knife at his thigh, though he'd love nothing more than to use his hands on these bastards.

He dug his boots into the mossy ground and met the heavier of the two sickos just outside the doorway, a man sandwiched between them. The big fella held the end of a metal rod the length of a broomstick away from his body, like a dogcatcher warding off the attacks of the mutt attached to the loop at its end. Only this time the mutt crawled naked on hands and knees from the black hole of the outhouse. Now that Street stood a few feet from its entrance he smelled it for what it was.

Mickey brought up the rear. His eyes alighted on Street. He guessed the guy wished he had his gun in his hands instead of his semi-erect penis. Street bore his gaze into Mickey's as he crushed his fist into the side of the first guy's head. His knuckles connected with the hinge of the man's jaw. A crack split the cool air and bone. The piece of shit howled like a ponce and hit the ground, taking the end of the stick with him.

A sickening number of shots erupted from the cabin. It took everything Street had not to run to Khani's aid. The continuous roll of an emptying clip gave him hope. She would never shoot wildly like that. And if her opponent needed that many shots, she was doing a hell of a job of staying out of the line of fire.

At Street's feet, a man of his own bulk gritted an old English curse, and then used the distraction to his advantage. His foot shot backward. Its impact folded Mickey's right knee in a beautifully unnatural position.

The fucker dropped his dick. Both his hands flew to his knee, but refrained from touching it. He squealed, and then teetered. The man on the ground helped him find it with a heel to the other shin.

Both of the prisoner's hands wrapped the pole and yanked it from beneath the big fella. The shit's jaw hung at an awkward angle, but he'd quit screaming and groped for his sidearm.

Street stood over the man. "Please, grab it."

He loosed a string of Russian.

A howl of pain equal to the bear's poured from the house. Street's lips tickled with a smile. That was his woman.

"I'm sorry, I didn't catch that," Street chuckled.

"Fuck you." The man pulled his gun.

Street bracketed his body atop the other man's. His hands cloaked the bloke's larger hands and wrestled the point of the barrel to the sicko's lop-sided jaw. "Not in this life."

He turned his head away and pulled the trigger. Arterial spray misted his neck.

A blast larger than the gunshot erupted from the cabin. It vibrated every nerve in Street's body. A void of sound enveloped him. No ringing here. He blinked down at the blood-spattered ground and the hole blasted out of the dead man's head.

On instinct, he rolled and pulled his sidearm.

The prisoner, presumably Zeke Slaughter, had removed the pole from his collar and beaten Mickey to death with it. The man would never make another high-pitched sound nor would he have the opportunity to violate another person.

Crimson speckled the prisoner who stumbled back as though completely spent. He braced his back against the shed and used the bloody pole to stay upright. His grey eyes blinked Street into focus. Lips shaped like Khani's formed words Street couldn't hear.

The thought of her jarred his addled brain. He lunged to his feet. "Khani!" Street guessed he screamed. The ringing came, but too loudly to make out anything else over it. "Khani!"

Ever pane of glass covered from the inside with thick drapes was now splintered into a thousand pieces. The covers hung errant from two of the windows and completely absent in another. Street rounded the front of the cabin at a full sprint. The door hung open by one hinge.

Khani's narrow frame lay sprawled on the scummy porch.

He slid to a stop at her side. "Khani!"

His hands hovered over her, afraid to touch her for fear of hurting her. She hadn't moved an inch, but from the back she didn't look injured. No blood. No misshapen limbs. Gingerly, he slipped two fingers against her neck.

Street stopped breathing. He might never inhale again. Desperately he repositioned his fingers.

Her pulse bumped the tips with even beats. "Thank you."

Movement caught his attention a split second before the cold barrel of a gun met his temple. Rage incinerated fear.

Booming toyed with his eardrums, but refused to let any sound inside his brain. His gaze lanced to the right. The dull ink of Russian tatts covered the wrist attached to the hand holding the gun. His right thumb lifted and jabbed the air, signaling him to rise.

"Blah blah blah blah," the man said. Or that's all he gleaned from the indeterminate noise.

"Can't hear shit." Street stood and met the guy face to face. He saw the pin attached to the silver chain circling the man's neck and the three-inch wound splitting his right pectoral. "Your fault, I'm guessing."

The bloke nodded. "Who are you?" He jammed the gun at his forehead front and center for emphasis.

Street still couldn't hear, but he read lips, faces, thoughts—almost before the person thought them. If this bastard couldn't get the information he wanted, Street would take Zeke's spot. The guy thought he could make Street talk. Furthermore, he wasn't ready to kill Street.

He moved before the man had time to think. Street stepped to the man, moving his head from the line of fire. His hands bracketed the son-of-a-bitch's nape and jaw, and then wrenched. Snap.

"I'm your end."

"Hey." A gruff voice whispered into Street's brain. He looked up and found Zeke clinging to the corner of the house, his gaze locked on Khani. "Is she…"

"No." Street barked the answer. "She'll be fine."

Yellow and green bruises covered Zeke's hefty body. Small round burns sprinkled his chest and legs. And the mother-fucking *inwardly* spiked choker still encompassed his neck.

"If you can make it, my pack is across the yard behind that third tree." Street pointed to the ruck. "I have clothes, food, water. If not—"

"I'll make it. Just take care of my sister."

"Don't you know your sister can take care of her damn self?" Both men swiveled to Khani's prone form. She glared at the corpse three feet from her. "You look better dead."

Street dropped to his knees beside her with the biggest dopiest grin on his face. A bruise gathered under her left cheek. He grazed his thumb over the area.

"Glad to see you could make it." Zeke hid his junk with both hands and winked the remnants of a black eye at Khani.

Tears gathered in her lifted gaze. She nodded and choked a laugh. "Glad to see you alive, even if you are butt naked."

"I'm going to take care of that." He turned away flashing his ass and a blue boot mark above his kidney.

"Those mother fuckers," Khani rumbled.

"...are all dead," Street supplied.

"Good fucking riddance."

She pushed herself off the porch. Her gaze traced Zeke across the distance to the rucksack where he tugged a pair of pants, ripped open a MRE, and downed an entire pack of M & M's and half a canister of water before looking for more clothes.

A hitch in her breath called his attention back to her. He offered his hand, giving her the option to take or leave it. Her hand clasped him and tugged him down. She encased him in her arms and squeezed hard enough to limit his oxygen intake.

"Thank you. I can never thank you enough for—" She choked on the words.

Street wrapped her in his arms, lifted her off the ground, and kissed her temple. "Sure you can. I have a great imagination."

She laughed so hard she clamped her side and groaned.

"Are you hurt?"

"It's nothing." She shooed away his concern with a swipe at her non-existent tears.

He set her on the floor and motioned for her to lift her shirt. "Nothing my keister. If that door hadn't opened to the outside, we wouldn't be having this argument."

She wiped beads of sweat from her brow. "You think this is an argument." Her mouth curved. "I thought you knew me better than that."

"Come on," he ordered with another flick of his wrist.

Her gaze jumped to Zeke who'd found a shirt and worked on demolishing the rest of the MRE, and then settled it on Street. She opened her jacket and lifted the hem of her T-shirt.

Street whistled long and low.

"What?" Her gaze leaped to her abdomen. Her muscled, milky-skinned, sexy as hell abdomen.

He moaned his appreciation.

Indignation dropped her jaw. "We're in the midst of a battle field and you're..." She shoved at his chest, and then grabbed his hand. "Come on. I hear the chopper."

"After being that close to the blast, how the hell can you hear anything?" *He* barely heard the whirling blades.

A dull black chopper complete with gunner in the door zipped over their heads on its way to the extraction point one click to the east where the trees stopped and the next patch of ice started.

"I guess we're both deaf." She tugged him behind her across the dead body and onto the ground.

They walked hand in hand to Zeke and Street had to check his glee at her open display of affection. This was hardly the time or place. Her brother was alive, but he'd been through some shit. And his body only told a portion of the story.

Khani dropped to her knees next to brother, leaned over and kissed the mop of hair on the top of his head.

"You might not want to do that. I smell like shit. Actual feces." The hunched man warned with a smile that hardly reached his mouth much less his stormy eyes.

"What the fuck is this?" Khani fingered the turn of the century torture device.

"My latest incentive to talk," Zeke croaked. He grabbed her hand. "Before you start yanking, I've tried it. There's no use. Its soldered closed."

"I'm sor—" Zeke held up his hand, muting Khani before she'd even gotten started.

"One time. You can say you're sorry one time, then never again. This wasn't your fault." Her brother's voice sounded rusty, as though he hadn't even used it to scream about whatever they'd done to him.

"I'm so sorry I didn't come with you. I'm sorry I didn't get here sooner. I'm sorry for wasting a year being pissed at you. I love you," Khani whispered.

Street's throat clogged at those three little words. Pussy. He didn't know if she'd ever said the words before. He sure as hell never expected to hear them slip from her lips. They were most definitely not directed at him. And yet, did he want them to be. Of course, he did. He couldn't believe it himself. But his entire life, hadn't he wanted to be loved? Who didn't?

Did Khani?

"I love you too, sis." Zeke said, not in reply but in the God's honest truth. That emotion reached the man's eyes and even lightened the weight folding his shoulders. Slowly the clouds returned to his demeanor. "I'm sure as hell glad you weren't with me. if they'd... I'm just glad you came when you did. Both of you." The grey gaze, larger, but no more intense than Khani's, hit Street's gaze.

"Me too," he nodded.

Zeke used both of the wet wipes in the utensil pack and wiped his hands as clean as the small sterile squares allowed. He held his hand out to Khani. When she put her hand in his he kissed the back of it, and then stood on wobbly legs. He thrust his hand at Street.

"Zeke, this is my," Khani swallowed. "This is the significant person in my life, King Street."

Both his and her brother's brows hit the sky.

"Call me, Street." He received and returned a sturdy warrior's handshake. "I'm really sorry."

One on Zeke's brows hit the deck, leaving one arched in question. Khani winced as if she knew what was coming.

"This is going to hurt like hell." Street lifted the man's handshake, lowered his shoulder, braced his left hand on Zeke's left thigh, and then hoisted him into a fireman's carry. The stalwart man didn't even breathe a groan, but then he didn't breathe at all for a long minute. "We have a mile to go. I'll make it as easy as possible."

Khani didn't have it easy. She toted both their packs to the plane, one on her front and one on her back. Neither did Zeke. His breath caught on each step, making Street wish it didn't take so many to get to the muster.

As expected the chopper awaited them at the exact coordinates. When they exited the tree line two men in dappled camo regs and light leather boots hit the deck. The airmen turned back, grabbed a green stretcher, and hustled toward them.

"You might want to hold your breath again," Street warned a few seconds before depositing him onto the litter. He took his pack from Khani and they hustled into the Hawk's belly.

Zeke held his head off the board to keep the spikes of the collar from piercing his skin.

"You have bolt cutters?" Street asked one of the airmen. The guy pointed behind him to a fastened metal box secured to the side of the Helo. He hurried to the container, tossed open the lid, and found the tool for the job.

Street slid on his knees in between two crewmembers fastening the gurney to the bird. He positioned the jaws on either side of the choker and pressed the handle together. It took three more bites of the cutters to break the contraption's hold. He eased the thing from around the man's large neck and threw it to the frozen ground below.

"Thank you," Zeke mouthed more than said. His white lips formed a hard line, expelling any blood flow from them. Grooves of pain carved his features into an unpleasant visage.

The power of freedom fled the man. Every jibe of the arduous hike must have jolted every injury with fresh misery. Street turned away in a crouch and motioned the medic over with a nod. "Can you give him something for the pain?"

"I'll have to check his vitals, but if I can, I will." The man scooted back to Zeke. His hands fastened a blood pressure cuff over his sleeved arm and then pressed two fingers onto the side of his wrist. The third airman worked to secure Zeke's IV.

Khani collapsed against the back frame of a flight chair, giving the crew room to work. Street took up post between her and the door and up they went. The trees shrank and the plane of ice grew impossibly large. Wind smacked their faces and ruffled their hair.

Several minutes into the flight Street noticed three dark specks against the white expanse. One large. Two small. He cradled Khani's hand in his. The move gently drew her attention from her brother's recumbent position. Her line of sight followed the point of his finger out the open helicopter door.

This close her laugh shook his ribs. "They look so friendly from this distance."

Street trained his gaze on Khani's face. It translated such strength and surprising vulnerability. "Yes, you do."

Chapter Twenty

The fight started at sixteen thousand feet.

A vicious curse knifed through the roar of the two turbo shaft engines, wind zipping past the closed doors at one hundred fifty knots, and King's boisterous snoring. Khani's eyes popped opened.

The medic spoke calmly. "I understand your concern. If they were my team, I'd be worried too. Before you can help them, you have to help yourself and let us get you better. As soon as we get to base, your friends can start the search." His arm, banded with white cloth and a red cross, lifted from Zeke and pointed toward her and King.

Her mouth opened to reassure her brother that they'd handle any problem as soon as the Hawk touched down at JBER—as the military dubbed Joint Base Elmendorf-Richardson. Zeke's balled fist shot up from the loosened strap of the stretcher. It connected with the medic's jaw, laying him flat.

The action roused the two soldiers sitting across from her. The nearest to the medic sprang to his aid, while the other wrestled with Zeke's free arm.

"Zeke." Khani straightened her back from King's shoulder.

"Stay where you are." The airman attending the medic who rolled about the floor clutching his jaw warned with a sharp finger. "Your Marine..." He jabbed the short nail at her. He must have recognized the commando dagger running laterally up Zeke's abdomen. When her gaze flew to it all she saw were new burn marks and bruises contorting the tattoo's precise lines. "He's being irrational."

That remained to be seen.

He continued, "Adrenaline combined with the reduction of his pain is making him feel up to task, wanting to complete the mission assigned him, no matter the cost. He could hurt you."

She snorted. "He's not my Marine. He's my brother."

Zeke arm-wrestled with the airmen who held the litter strap in the air, ready to secure his wrist. If only he could get the upper hand on a man beaten, malnourished, and anchored to the floor of a helicopter. Grunts snarled from her brother's mouth. The younger, smaller soldier panted.

"Bloody hell." King shifted behind her.

Khani ignored all the men, but Zeke. She crawled to his side. "Zeke. Stop fighting and talk to me."

"Tell them to let me go." Veins bulged in her brother's pale forehead. They created a catacomb across his battered neck, arms, and chest.

"Tell me what's wrong," she ordered.

"I can't," he shouted so loudly it cracked her eardrums. "You'll try and fix it. It'll make things worse." Zeke freed his other hand. He added it to the struggle. The added strength helped him pry the airman's arm over his punished torso. The young man screeched in pain.

"Stop. You're going to break his arm." She hollered the word. Her arm shot out to disengage Zeke's hold.

Her brother's left hand released the airman and clamped around her throat. "Let me go."

The move stunned more than hurt. Her hands flew to his wrist, but she barred the instinct to fight. She stared at the IV line hanging from the ceiling and tried to wrap her head around what was happening.

King's fist flew across the space. A thud slackened Zeke's grip. Air returned to Khani's lungs. She fell back on her ass. The airman did also, clutching his arm to his stomach. She stared from her unconscious brother to King's tight expression. "Thank you. It needed doing." And she couldn't have done it.

He bowed his head, fixed Zeke's wrists back in the Velcro cuffs, and then sat between them. "You fellas all right?"

"All, but my pride." The medic sat on his arse between the other two; both nodded in accession. "I should've seen it coming. Especially with his," he paused and lowered his voice, "apparent captivity and torture. Who the hell would want to be restricted after what he's been through? Not me, for sure."

"What reason did he give you for wanting to be released?" Khani asked.

"I assumed he was talking out of his head about you two." His shoulders bobbed. "Now I know better. He's worried about the fate of his team. Said he needed to warn them of danger immediately."

She looked to King. His locked jaw and steady gaze gave away none of his thoughts. "If they're in danger, why couldn't we help warn them? Why does it have to be him?"

"I don't know." King's voice was cool, distant. He stared into near space. His mossy eyes were calculating something he wasn't ready to share, which only ramped her curiosity. She expected him to say more. When he didn't she stared down at her brother, seeking answers that wouldn't come. Not for the next ten minutes or more.

"We're on approach," the airman who'd avoided injury announced.

A collective breath released cabin pressure.

They touched down five minutes later, greeted by a short man in a matching speckled uniform, save for the eagle embroidered into his hat.

"Colonel. We're in your debt." She and King both extended their hands.

The man snorted. "Debt. I still owe Tucker a few favors before I get mine paid off. Hell, I'm happy to help. I never thought I'd see the day I got to repay even a fraction of the grace that sneaky son of a bitch showed me."

He shook their hands in turn, and then waved them toward his monstrous truck. "We'll follow the boys to the hospital, where Dr. Valentine will meet us. You can talk to her, and then whenever you're ready, I'll take you to an open officer's barrack. It's not the Ritz, but it's warm and dry. I've had some clothes and food stocked for you. However long you need us, we're at your disposal."

King gestured for her to go first and followed her to the vehicle. To his credit he didn't offer her a boost into the cab, but he should've given the Colonel the option. The man's left leg remained straight, impeding his ascent into the driver's seat. "Don't worry. My right one works perfectly, my left one is still attached, and my ticker is still ticking thanks to Tucker."

He strapped on his safety belt and waited for them to do the same before following the white and red truck through the level streets for only two straightaways
and three turns. They met at the back of a large tan complex.

As he'd said a woman with feathery bangs, a bun pinned at her nape, and a white coat rushed the lead truck. A man and woman in scrubs followed suit with a rolling gurney, ready to take over for the airman.

Khani's throat clogged at the sight of Zeke's marred body being lifted out of the truck bed. He was alive and he'd be back to peak condition in no time. And still, she coughed against her raw emotions.

She and King kept silent as they exited the vehicle and followed the bed, being rolled toward sliding doors by the medical team.

When they reached the door a nurse held up her hand. "I'm sorry, you can't come back here. If you'll walk around to—"

"They're clear," Dr. Valentine hollered from ten feet down the hall. "Put them in my office. I'll be with you as soon as I have something to report." Her feet continued their rapid chop down the corridor, and then her brother and his entourage disappeared around a corner.

Looking sheepish, the older lady led them through a maze of doors and into the neatest office she'd ever seen.

"Whoa," King exclaimed. It was the first thing he'd said since the Helo. No jokes. No male bravado. No sexual innuendoes. No King Street.

"Yeah, Dr. Valentine is extremely tidy. No one is allowed in her office. Not even her husband. Not her staff. Especially not her kids. You two must be royalty or something." The nurse moved to close the door, but stopped. "Royalty or not, I wouldn't touch anything, if I were you. We might have to roll you out of this place in a body bag." She smiled, and then closed them into a veritable prison.

Khani paced from one side of the alphabetized bookshelf with perfectly aligned spines to the other. She didn't dare look at King for fear of what he'd say or not say. Something ate at him. It showed in his silence and missing humor. It showed in the way he avoided her gaze, avoided touching her.

An hour in, she didn't know which she toiled with more, her brother's problem that was so twisted he couldn't talk to her about or what King had to say to her.

Chapter Twenty-one

Zeke had broken ribs, was dehydrated and weak from malnourishment, but would recover quickly. The doctor had insisted on keeping him sedated through the night to minimize risk to himself and others. They'd been ushered out of her office and into the colonel's hands with only a low grumble about the track Khani had worn in the carpet.

Street nodded his thanks to the high-ranking man indebted to Vail Tucker and headed for the barracks door. He slid the key into the lock. It opened into a twelve-foot square with stale air and no more furnishings than the cabin had after the explosion that nearly ended the life of his woman. A woman that slipped through his fingers before he had the chance to firm his grasp.

With a flip of the wall switch a florescent box light splitting the living area-slash-kitchen flickered to life. He tossed the keys onto the counter a few feet away, dropped both their rucks to the right of the entry, and headed to the only door besides the mini closet door in the kitchen.

A full-sized bed with crisp blue linens lay beyond the thin wall. The precise corners looked sharp enough to cut flesh. It would just beat sleeping on the floor if Khani knocked him unconscious, which could very well happen.

His foot hit the threshold of a bare bones shower and shitter when the front door hit the frame with a resounding thud. A small part of him cringed, while the rest of him tugged up trousers and turned to meet his fate.

Colonel must have packed the cheerful grin Khani had given him and taken it with him. Her jacket lay on the ground. His did too for that matter. He'd forgotten the damn thing in the truck.

A surly scowl drew her features taut. Her fingers pinched her narrow hips. She hitched both brows to her hairline and tilted her head with a quick snap. His cock twitched in response to her unspoken command.

He didn't breath.

He'd clocked Zeke without asking questions. The man's hand had been clamped around Khani's throat. Her brother should feel lucky he'd shown such restraint. Anyone else would've been pitched out of the Hawk with his arms flapping and all the prayers left in his lungs.

Street hadn't known why the bloke freaked. It hadn't mattered. Only it mattered a hell of a lot. Zeke Slaughter might be a mercenary punk, but he was a loyal one. Over days of torture—the world of which didn't show on his tattered body—he hadn't broken. He'd kept his mission's, his teammates', his command's confidence at all cost.

Now that he was free he needed to protect those vulnerable to the crime syndicate. His team. His friends. He would stop at nothing to get to them. To warn them against danger.

Only Street knew it was too late.

Stas had already taken them. The mob had already started torturing them. In order to keep

Zeke from ripping the IV out of his vein and stumbling off to save the day when he'd only get himself killed, Street had to tell the man what he knew.

He had to explain to Khani that he'd betrayed her trust. That he'd gone behind her back and researched her brother and her.

In order to save her from losing the only person on earth she loved, he had to give her up. He had no doubt in his mind that she'd force him out of her life...forever.

"Spit it out," she ordered, breaking the stony silence.

His gaze narrowed.

"Don't play dumb." Khani speared a finger at him from across the distance.

Desperation steamed the blood in his veins. It mingled with the desire to hold onto her forever.

"You haven't said two words since we landed. You've avoided my eyes, even my ass." She scoffed. "Whatever you have to say," her arms spread wide, "out with it already."

His voice was rusty and thick, the words clear. "I love you."

Her chest flinched visibly in the white thermal shirt molded to her every muscle, gentle curves, and the stiff tips of her nipples. If he'd barreled across the room and blown into her sternum, he couldn't have knocked the wind out of her more thoroughly. That truth read clearly on her slacked jaw and wide eyes.

"It's not possible," she wheezed.

"Sure it is. You're easy to love."

"The hell I am," she bit, regaining a bit of her footing. "I'm mean and irritable. I bite your head off on a daily basis, and I'm not the kind of lover you enjoy."

"You're a no bullshit kind of woman." He took a step forward. "Your resolve excites me. Your vulnerability disarms me." When she didn't bolt he took another step and then another bringing him toe to toe with his undoing. He skimmed a finger over her strong jaw. "And we both know I quite enjoy you as a lover."

Street grabbed her hands and secured them behind his neck. That innocent contact stroked his length to full erection. "I don't need you to accept it. I don't need you to love me back. I needed you to know I love you, Khani." He bent and rested his forehead against hers. "And I need you right now more than I ever have. Fuck me, before I forget myself and nail you to the door."

"Do it," she barked. Her breath caressed his hungry mouth.

"Do what exactly?" he ground, holding onto the strings of his restraint.

"Grab my ass, impale me with your big dick, and screw me to the door, now."

It wasn't a declaration of love. He hadn't expected one. But this was as close to surrender as Khani Slaughter would ever come. Right or wrong with his secret between them, he'd take it with greedy thrusts.

As answer, he snatched the hem of her shirt and yanked it over her head. She pulled her arms from his neck and through the sleeves. No bra. The petite pink points of her breasts demanded his ardent gaze and more. She harangued him without words, jerking his belt free. His hips shot forward, eagerly grinding into her flat palm.

A groan detonated in his craned neck, but the persistence of his lust drove him. He tussled with the button of her pants and zipper. Once over her hips the loose-legged pants fell to the floor.

He dropped to his knees in front of her. The laces on her boots took precious time to unlace, but he didn't squander the seconds. His gaze lifted to her crotch, and then her eyes in question.

"Yes, King," she sighed.

His name on her lips was the closest he'd ever get to heaven. Well, his name on her lips when she came from his thrusts. His teeth nipped at her lace panties. Her hips bowed. He tongued her through the material, catching tastes of her flesh through the netted fabric.

Too soon her laces came undone. Her panting said she was also close to coming undone. Good. He didn't want to hurt her. He would, but only to protect her. Maybe she'd know that much.

Street tugged her boots and socks off her feet. He stood, shucked his shirt, unfastened the line of buttons on his pants, pushed everything over his hips, filled his hands with her lush bottom, and then hoisted her into the air. Her arms locked around his neck and pulled him to her breasts.

His fingers hooked into her panties. With a wrench the material moved, granting the crown of his head access to her silken skin.

Shirt suffocating him, pants around his ankles, he plowed into her tight little channel. She screamed into the barren room. Her heels dug into his ass. He held completely still for an interminable minute.

"Pump me onto you. Make me fuck you, lover." Her words came hot in his ear.

He followed orders like he had special training for it. His fingers dug into her flesh. Up. He pulled her to the tip of his shaft. Down. He released her weight and rammed deep. Up and down he drove them both until sweat beaded on his forehead from gritting his restraint.

She licked a line up the side of his neck. "More," she demanded.

He stepped forward, pinning her back to the door. His hands slid to the crooks of her knees. He lifted them high, changing the angle.

Now his thrusts fucked her, screwing her into the door as promised. Like she wanted. Like he needed.

Street let go of tomorrow. He focused on her keening breaths, on her slick, lithe body, on her screaming pleasure. And he released his.

Chapter Twenty-two

Street dragged his feet all the way to the hospital, through the corridors, and up the elevator. Maybe she'd screwed the pep right out of his step. She'd gone at him like a women possessed, taking control after his confession had rendered her incapable of speech. Of all the things she'd expected him to say, love was last on the list.

Letting him take the lead once or twice in the sack was an entirely different thing than declaring her love. No question, she loved the man. As much as she'd tried to deny it, there was no refuting the evidence.

Damn it.

But he deserved better than her. Yes, she was great in the sack, would never turn into a middle-aged marshmallow, and could keep up with him on any battlefield, but she couldn't—no—*wouldn't* give him children. And he would make a great father.

She stared at his profile, willing him to look at her, to say those words that she shouldn't want to hear again. The words that shouldn't mean so much to her. He stared at the flashing red numbers at the top of the shiny silver door, a veil of resignation clouding his mood. Was it because— other than hollered orgasms and orders—she hadn't said much after his confession?

Her gaze hit the floor. She gnawed on her lower lip, missing the tang of her signature lip colors. For maybe the first time ever, Khani didn't check her make-up in the reflection. She hadn't applied the stash she kept next to her extra ammo in her bag. Only after she'd been covered in Vail's blood and unwilling to leave his side for fear he'd utter the name of his attacker, had she been clean faced in public. The last few days in the middle of nowhere without it made the discomfort bearable.

King's gaze, his wise and understanding eyes, would ease her self-consciousness, but he remained sober and staring ahead.

The elevator dinged. The doors opened.

Zeke stood in the gap.

Stood was an exaggeration. He listed as though he were the tenuous flame of a birthday candle. A hospital gown flapped around his hairy knees. His breaths labored in pants, threatening to buckle his own legs. Blood dripped from the top of his hand onto the white inlayed rubber floor. It streamed from the vein where an IV had been less than a minute ago.

"Going someplace?" Khani asked.

"They discharged me. I just didn't feel like hanging around while they did paperwork." Zeke heaved.

"And I peed standing this morning." She jabbed her finger toward the corridor. "Back to bed, Zeke."

"No." He snapped and straightened to his full height, which was well over her head.

A growl rumbled from King's throat.

"I reserved myself yesterday, Zeke. So help me, if you make one false move in my direction I'll lay you out with no help from him." She took one bold step out of the elevator. Her brother stepped backward, or tried. His right leg gave and he pitched toward the ground.

She reached out for his hand, but King hooked his arm under Zeke's pit. "Blast it, your sister isn't nearly this eager for me to sweep her off her feet." He hefted her bother over his shoulder. "This makes twice. One more time and I might get flattered."

Khani couldn't hold back her chuckle. Zeke glared at her from King's broad back. A back she'd gripped so hard last night it had eight perfect crimson nail marks this morning that hid under the navy of the borrowed Air Force T-shirt. Luckily the temperature had taken an upswing during the night. Colonel sent their dirty jackets and clothes to the laundry before dropping them off.

A blonde nurse skidded to a stop around the corner. Her hand covered her heart. "Thank goodness. He's been a pain in my a...he's been a challenge all morning."

"All morning? It's not even daylight yet," Khani pointed out.

"We'll he's an early riser," the forty-something woman explained as she rushed ahead of them to the *im*patient's room. She stood at the doorway and ushered them in with a flourish.

King stopped and let Khani lead the way into the sterilized room. She scooted close to the sink, making room for the caravan to come. Then King and Zeke filled the threshold. Then he turned and pushed the door toward the frame. "We're going to need a few minutes alone."

Before the befuddled nurse responded, he thrust the door in her face. King walked to the hospital bed and plunked her brother down on his bare backside. Zeke hissed for an eight count, and then split his angry gaze between her and King, who took up watch at the window.

"Look." Khani rested her hands on her hips. "I have the resources to locate your teammates and protect them until the threat is eliminated, which I can also handle. You don't need to warn them in person. In fact, you can pick up the bloody phone and achieve the same outcome."

"I told you yesterday, you—the organization you work for—cannot be involved with the people I work for." He sat, but propped his shoulder against the bed's railing.

"Why not?" Khani asked the same question she'd needed to know yesterday.

"I can't tell you," Zeke said without compunction.

She folded her arms and squeezed her fists together. "I can help you."

"No, you can't. Not this time. Your help will only hurt." Zeke's grey eyes mirrored an all-too-familiar determination. "And I've done nothing but call their numbers since I regained consciousness." His gaze sliced to King's back silhouetted against the clear sky and scruffy green treetops. "No answer. That doesn't mean anything. They won't answer. A strict no-communication policy went into effect as soon as our mission went live."

"They won't answer because Stas already has them."

Khani stared at King's back as the word seeped into her brain. *They won't answer because Stas already has them.*

Chapter Twenty-three

"You assume." Khani stated it as fact. If only that were true.

Street turned to face her. "I know," he said simply, but it was the most complex thing he'd ever said in his life. Even more involved than his confession of love. This was the proof of his devotion. She would never see it that way, but he knew.

He looked to Zeke. The man held up an impenetrable facade, except for the flare of his nostrils. "Your friends, Greer Britton and Derrick Coen, were reported missing four days ago."

"You know?" she asked in a trill. When his gaze drifted back to Khani, her dark brows drew tightly over turbulent eyes. "How do you know?"

"I used our resources to research Zeke's background, who he worked for, when, where," he explained.

The definitive news wilted Zeke onto the bed.

"When?" Instead of yelling, her word whispered across the distance that seemed to expand with the seconds that ticked by.

"You wouldn't open up to me. You wouldn't share. I told you I refused to go into a situation blind for all our sakes." Street held his ground, afraid any advance or tender gesture would intensify the stand-off.

"So it's my fault you snuck behind my back, and then lied to me about it while getting me to fuck you again?" she spat.

Zeke groaned.

He ignored her brother. The piece of shit didn't know how lucky he was to have Khani's unfettered love and devotion. "No. I knew what I was doing every step of the way. If I had it to do over again, I would. All of it."

"Yeah." The muscles in her jaw flexed. "I'll bet you would." Her head jerked as though the sight of him repulsed her. "You sure fucked me, didn't you?"

"I tried to protect you." He broke and took a step in her direction.

Khani sidestepped, backing her shoulders to the sink. "Leave."

Street retreated the step and lifted his palms in surrender. "I'll leave when you're both home safely. You don't have—"

She cut him off with a slice of her bladed hand through the air. "You said you'd never hurt me. I knew you were a lot of things, but not a liar."

The comment hit him square between the eyes. Being called a liar was nothing new. She wasn't the first to say it. She wouldn't be the last. But he'd hurt her. His troop admitted as much, which said a lot about how much she'd opened up to him over the last few days. It said a lot about what an idiot he was.

Tears glimmered in her eyes. They fueled her rage. She blinked wildly, crossed to the door, and opened it. "Leave now."

Chapter Twenty-four

Was there anything more irritating than a commercial flight? Plenty came to mind, but none more boisterous and close to her stinging eardrum than Zeke. She'd done a great job of ignoring him over the past two days and close-contact eight hours. It wasn't hard to ignore someone when they were unconscious. Try ignoring them stuffed into the seat next to you in a tiny double row at sixty-thousand feet. It took so much effort she'd shaved a few centimeters off her molars.

His attempted escape combined with the scathing words he had for the head nurse who found a new vein, restarted his IV, and explained the stringent rules of the facility, had earned him round the clock sedation until the doctor released him. His induced coma had given her plenty of time to see that the Polzins didn't leave their cell for a good long time, along with their cop buddy who'd taken their bribes.

The cabin attendant propped a hip against the seat, jarring her from the darkness of her mind. "We're on approach. Can I get you anything else? Another pack of—"

"No, thank you." Khani shooed the woman away with a wave. Zeke's mouth gaped and his eyes followed the shiny snack packs in her hands as she moved to the row behind them, where she collected empty cups. At least it shut him up for a second. But just one.

"I can't bloody believe you let those wankers dope me while my friends are..." His gaze shot around the cabin of the Boeing. "I can't bloody believe it."

Khani canted her head toward him, giving him her full attention for the first time in the eleven long hours he'd been awake and rattling on about the same damn thing over and over. The fight finally fled him. He plowed long fingers into his dark mop and twisted them into the nap. True misery haunted his eyes.

Her defenses clattered the earth. "If you'd gone off fully cocked with no ammunition, they'd have killed you along with your friends."

"Put yourself in my position." He leaned so close his nose bumped her cheek. The touch annoyed her because it made her think about the last person to caress her face, the only person. "Put your precious Branch operatives in jeopardy, and then think about what you'd do in my position." He eased back into his seat and mumbled, "I can't bloody believe it."

"You can't believe I would put your life above that of your friends?"

Khani remembered the time he'd found a half-broken harmonica on the side of the road. He'd played that damn thing for days on end, driving her to the front steps of the looney bin. She hadn't taken it away, tossed it into the road and clapped as traffic smashed it into bits. He'd been a child with no toys to call his own. She'd gritted her teeth and endured.

But he was no longer a child.

"I put your life above my own. Hell yes, I'd put it above your friends."

"It's time for you to stop." Every ounce of bitterness faded from his voice. Mature finality emanated in his tone.

Was he pushing her away? After all they'd been through. After all they'd survived together, how could he close her out of his life? His friends apparently meant more to him than she did.

Zeke sighed a long drawn breath.

She just blinked at him to keep the waterworks in check—something she did quite often over the last few days. *Fucking pansy.*

"Khan." He grabbed both her hands into his palm and shielded them with his right. "You've always looked out for me, always put me first and still do. I remember every time you went without dinner so I could eat. You collected bottles constantly, turning them in for a tiny fraction of a pound. And when you finally collected enough to buy clothes from a second-hand store, you bought me a harmonica to replace the broken one I'd dropped down the sewer grate the week before."

He smiled. "After all these years, it's my most prized possession."

"I thought that was your 'Cuda," she said, reminding him of the 1970 cherry red muscle car he'd bought upon arrival in the States.

Zeke sucked a breath through his teeth. "It's a close one, but Elizabeth comes in second."

"Elizabeth?"

He shrugged, and then grimaced. "She's royalty."

"Queen Elizabeth." Khani's head shook.

The smile curving his lips fell. "I moved to the States for a job, but I also took it for the distance it would put between us."

She tugged her hands back, needing them to temper the ache of her already shredded heart.

Zeke held firm. "I hated the thought of being away from you, but I thought if we were apart, you'd make a life for yourself that didn't revolve around caring for me. And then..."

"And then I followed you across the pond," she finished.

"Yeah," he said, looking chagrinned. "I never expected you'd leave England. When you did, I stayed away for a few reasons. The biggest of them being my hope that you'd start living." His hand closed around hers. "And you did."

Khani turned her head away and found two wet-eyed women wedging their heads so hard into the gab between the seats they'd need the Jaws of Life to extract them. Their clumpy lashes spread wide in surprise. They snapped around and faced the cockpit. Guess they didn't need help after all.

"Khan." Zeke tugged on her hands, but she looked past the guilty women to a row of middle-aged men trying not to touch elbows in the narrow seats.

"I had a hunch about why you left home. Now I know I'm too smart for your own good."

"Shut it," she said.

"You have no one to blame, but yourself. Should have let me shirk on my homework once or twice a week."

Finally she relented and gave him her tired gaze.

"You love him." Zeke's lips pursed.

"Sod it all, yes."

"He loves you."

She didn't dignify that with a response. Unless a huff qualified as a response.

"Khani," he urged. "Did you learn nothing from our dispute?"

"That's different."

"You wasted a year being mad at me for wanting to protect you."

"I wasted a year being mad at you for your dishonesty. He knew how I felt about honesty from the very first, long before he betrayed me."

"Which goes to show how much he cares about you."

"When we get to DC you're getting another MRI. I think Valentine missed something."

"He knew if you lost me, you'd be devastated. You told me earlier that if he hadn't been there, steering your efforts, you wouldn't have found me. Whatever he learned in his research was critical to my rescue, but if you'd known about it sooner you'd have pushed him away. It's what you do, even to me."

When she started to look away Z pressed her hands flat between his palms. "He didn't have to come clean. You'd have never known, but he also knew I'd have done anything to get to my friends in time to warn them. He also knew I would have gotten myself into an elephant's backside of trouble."

Zeke grinned—something he wasn't prone to. "He loves you more than he loves himself, sis. Now you have to figure out how to deal with that truth."

He released her hands. The airplane zipped over the clouds. She stared at them for a long time, hours, thinking about every conversation she and King had over the course of the trip. Remembering every touch. Every look.

As hard as it was, she turned her scrutiny inside, to the ugly truth she never wanted to sully herself with.

She'd taken care of Zeke for so long he became her shield to the world. She hid behind him and in turn clung to the past.

Khani had done what she always did and pushed King away. She'd hurt the man she loved. She'd shunned a man accustomed to the world's neglect. His own mother had abandoned him. Yet, he'd put his trust in her.

And she fucked up.

Her ears popped several times as they descended into Reagan National. Khani grabbed her carry-on and waited in the mid-plane shuffle with Zeke at her back. Slowly, they made their way to the luggage carousel for her three bags.

She swallowed the rise of emotion and turned to her bother. How he'd grown from the scrawny kid she incessantly worried didn't get enough to eat into a beautiful man. She didn't agree with his career choice, but hey, at least he had a job, a house, a car, and a mission...whatever it may be. She wrestled him into an embrace, squeezing as hard as she dared with his cracked ribs.

"I love you, Zeke." When she thought her heart would burst she released him and stepped back. "I'll see you later, okay?"

"What?" His chin dropped and he looked at her down his nose.

"Beat it. You don't have any luggage."

"You're not putting me in cuffs?" he asked with a lopsided smirk.

"No. You were right. It's time I let go of the past, take care of myself, and let you take care of yourself. So," she clutched his hand, "take care of yourself."

He smashed her hand in his. "I will, sis. You taught me how." His fingers slipped though hers. He turned and trotted out the sliding glass doors.

Khani watched him flag a cab and hop in as though he had the world to save. The yellow car eased into traffic and the brother she worked so hard to save disappeared into the trickling traffic.

The pang she expected to stab her in the center of her heart was replaced by hope. The next weeks wouldn't be easy, but she knew what she needed to do.

Chapter Twenty-five

It had taken less time than expected to get everything in order in DC. Her boys found Cara Lee. And she'd judiciously left Vail in charge of that explosive situation. She had more important business to attend to.

One month and twelve days after she left Anchorage, Khani walked into the office of the commander of the Base Branch's London division—her old office.

"I knew you were coming and I still can't believe my eyes." Baine McCord's rich bass rumbled across the room. He stood from his desk, from the mounds of files and errant papers, and strode around the side.

"I can't believe you're the freaking commander." She hurried across the distance and tossed her arms around her friend.

After several seconds his arms tentatively encompassed her. "You want the job, say the word and it's yours. Too much damn paperwork and too many meetings."

"Not a chance." She settled her heels onto the floor and looked up at his clean-shaven face. "Never thought I'd see the day you'd lose the beard."

"Tell me about it. Alma and Alisa eyed me like an imposter for days." He chuckled. "Never thought

I'd see the day you'd hug me." His light eyes twinkled with his smile. "What do they put in the water over there?" He nodded his head in the direction of the States. "I've known you for what, almost twenty years? And you've never even offered a hand shake."

"I'm working on some personal shit," she explained.

"Aren't we all."

"Speaking of personal, how are your ladies?"

"Come sit." He directed her to one of the two chairs opposite his and he took the other. Well, his smile took up most of the chair. "They're expensive. Why do you think I came back to the job?"

"Because you love making a difference." Khani looped her heavy tote on the arm of the chair.

"There's that too." He nodded. "Two weeks ago we celebrated the girl's fifth birthday. And if Sloan has her way, we'll have a little boy's birthday to celebrate next year."

"What? Are you trying to..." she stalled, realizing how inappropriate the question was.

"Adoption," he supplied. "He's the cutest damn thing, but he's tiny, squish-able." Baine pulled a phone from his pocket and punched some numbers. A fat grin spread across his face. "Look." He offered her the view of the screen and the swaddled grub displayed across it. "I don't know what do with a baby."

"When they came into your life you didn't know what to do with the girls. You'll figure this out in no time. They're not near as breakable as they look."

"Let's hope not." Baine stowed his phone and eased back into the chair with a baffled look cramping his face. "Now, before I give you the key to the building, so to speak, I need to make sure I understand something. You want me to demote you?"

"Yes." She crossed her leg and sat forward.

"You know you used to bark orders at me, right?" he reminded.

"Not that you listened." She grinned.

"True enough." He rubbed his chin, an obvious throwback from his bearded days. "Just tell me why."

"It goes back to that personal shit," she offered.

"You and Street?" he prodded.

"Absolutely."

He nodded. "I can't say I understand it, but I don't need to. All I need to see is the peace on your face. When will you see Law? Because I can't keep this a secret for much longer."

"Are you guys free for dinner tomorrow?" she asked. "I could tell him then."

"Are you cooking?"

"It's been a long time, but yeah. I'll cook for old friends."

"Then we're free." He grinned.

"Great. All of you at my new flat around seven?"

"It's a date." Baine smacked a fist on the arm of his chair, and then rounded his desk. He closed his laptop and stuffed it into a briefcase. Then he hefted the phone. "You sure you're ready for this? He's been a beast around here the last few weeks. I've threatened to knock him down to size more than once."

"I'm sure." She nodded.

"Just clean up the blood before you leave." Baine lifted the phone from the cradle and depressed a single button. "Street, my office in three." He grimaced. "Your date can wait for an hour."

Khani took the punch like a professional. She gagged and hacked and cried on the inside. Outside she didn't blink. Of course he'd moved on. She hadn't spoken to him in a month and her last words to him were harsh enough he'd be justified if he chose to ignore her appeal.

Baine replaced the receiver, rounded the desk with his briefcase in tow, and reached for her hand. He placed a kiss on the back of her hand. "For better or worse, I'm glad you're back, and I'm glad you're trying."

"Thank you, Commander." She managed a smile. "Better or worse, I'm happy to be back."

He released her hand. "See you tomorrow night, and then Monday morning, Operative Slaughter." Baine bowed his head, and then headed for the door. He headed right out of it, away from Street's office.

Khani stood, smoothed her sweaty palms down her black skirt, and then faced the door. The seconds that ticked seemed the longest in her life. Longer than when she searched for Zeke. Longer than the hours spent waiting for daylight on London's streets.

She waited for calm to descend like it always did before an op. It remained stubbornly out of reach of her trembling fingers.

The door swung wide. "I've got shit to..." Two steps inside the door, King's hazel gaze froze on her.

"King," she whispered.

He just stared for an interminable minute.

She took the time to study his thick legs and wide shoulders the well-tailored suit barely contained. Her gaze drank in his chin and narrowing hazel gaze. Those speckled eyes swept the room, likely looking for his boss. When they didn't find anyone else in the office they settled back on her.

"Khani, you're looking well," he said with maddening reserve.

"Cut the bull," she snapped. "I didn't cross half the world for polite conversation."

His mouth tightened as though fighting back words, words she wished he'd set free. She probably didn't want to hear all of what he had to say, but it beat his constraint. "Okay," he said.

Okay? She deserved that and more. After all she'd brought them here. She straightened her shoulders and dragged in a breath. "Have you found someone else?"

"What?" His brows knitted.

"Your date," she reminded. "You don't owe me any kind of explanation. But I'd like to know before I continue."

He rubbed a hand over his close-cropped hair. "Continue what? I'm not especially soft in the head, but I have no idea what's going on right now."

"I need to apologize." Khani took a step forward. King's large hand flew up, palm out. The back-off gesture stopping her cold.

"My date is with Callie...my dog. I've only had her for a week. I haven't told anyone because I didn't know if she'd keep me."

The sentiment broke her heart all over again. He was worried the dog would reject him. Fucking hell, everyone else had...even her. If she hadn't been in intensive therapy with a top-notch shrink over the last month, she'd hate herself right now. But that wouldn't do either of them any good.

"She slept on my pillow last night." He struggled. "I guess that means we're solid."

"I've always wanted a dog, but when I got older, I didn't want the responsibility."

"It's a pain in the ass, walking at all hours." His gaze hit his shoes, and then slowly bounced back to hers. "You don't need to apologize, Khani. You were right. I should have told you and let the chips fall, but..." His throat bobbed on a swallow. "Betrayal is what I do. History proves as much. You need to be with someone who you can place your trust in one hundred percent."

"That person is you, King."

An uncharacteristic frown curved his lips. "It's not."

"What history?" she begged in a whisper.

"Father Tommy." He stuffed his hands into his pockets.

"The man who took you in? The priest?"

His head bobbed. "Yep. He took me in and I betrayed him." The bob turned into a shake. King's gaze bore into hers. "He killed himself because of my treason."

"Not because of you," she matched his shaking head.

"You have no idea." He gave a caustic laugh.

"King, you do what's right, no matter the cost."

"Sometimes the cost should come into play." He extricated his hands from his pockets and clasped them together. "I'm sorry you came all this way for an apology you didn't need to give." The front of his wingtips lifted as though he were about to turn away and leave.

"I'm not just visiting and I didn't just come for the apology."

His tips hit the ground. "You moved back to London?" His gaze rounded the room. "Are you taking my job or what?"

"I'm not taking your job," she explained. "Actually, you're my boss."

That got a little slack jaw, at least a second of one. "Why would you take a demotion?"

"It's my surrender."

"Why would you surrender? It's not your way."

"I want to be under you in some way. I can't be under you in the bedroom, but I can give you this."

"You don't need to give me anything." Again he held up his hands. He took a step toward the door.

Khani used the point of her stiletto to hook the leg of the chair Baine had sat in and turned it to face King. "Get in the chair."

His hands fell and his shoulders drew straight. "I thought I was *your* boss?"

"Tomorrow. Now move," she barked.

His gaze shifted from her to the chair and back several times. "Khani, I—"

She slipped her hand inside her tote and yanked out the black leather strap with a matching black silicone ball at its center. "Has anyone ever told you that you talk too much?"

His lids widened. "This one bird told me something like that."

"The next thing I pull from my bag won't be so innocuous."

"You call that mundane?" He pointed at the ball-gag.

"King Street, put your ass in the chair."

"What about Baine?"

"The only thing you need to worry about is me."

He regarded her with each step toward the metal-framed chair. When he reached it he turned and sat. The leather creaked under his weight.

The last of Khani's apprehension fled. Desire and love enveloped her chest. "Open wide." King's lips parted slowly. She placed the small ball between his teeth. "Close. This is a training ball. It shouldn't strain your jaw...too much," she added with a smirk.

She fastened the buckle at the back of his head and moved to her bag. His wide eyes and protracted lips followed her every move. Next she pulled out four thick leather cuffs. "I can't have you running out on me."

Khani knelt in front of him and secured his ankles and then wrists to the chair. King's nostrils flared. His breaths increased. She placed her hand over his knees.

King's gaze fused with hers.

"From the first time I laid eyes on you, I knew you were the worst kind of trouble." She skimmed her palms up his thighs. "You made me embrace a danger I'd never allowed into my personal life. You made me feel, period. Joy. Unparalleled sexual euphoria. Peace. Anger. Frustration. Elation. Heartbreak."

His eyes mirrored the emotions she listed.

Her hands coasted up his chest. She settled them over his heart.

"But most of all... You made me love you." He blinked. She continued. "I love you, King Street. I have for so long, but I was scared. I was scared of losing you, of my own vulnerability." She stood and kissed his forehead, his cheeks, his chin. "I pushed you away because it was easier than looking inside of myself, than letting go of my demons. I'm a work in progress, but I want to work on it with you."

She leaned back. "What do you say?"

His head canted and his gaze dropped to the gag.

Khani smiled, and then released the buckle.

He studied her tote. "What else do you have in that bag?"

She lightly pinched his nipple, but laughed along with his wine rich chuckle.

King's mouth brushed her cheek. She turned to face him and their mouths tangled in an intimate embrace. "I love you, Khani. I'll always want you. I'll always love you."

Always? There was one more point she had to make and it hurt her heart even though right now it was the truth and he needed to know it before they moved forward. "I can't give you babies." She lifted her chin, stealing her touch, but giving the full force of her gaze. "I raised Zeke. I'm done. I can't handle that kind of vulnerability again. You deserve babies, beautiful, hazel eyed babies."

"I want you. Not babies. Who knows what kind of blood runs in my veins? I don't. Besides, I wouldn't know what to do with a baby." He smirked.

"You would make a great papa." She swallowed.

"Callie might object. I haven't gotten her outside in time to pee all week. She's made a mess of my rug." He scowled. "I hope my dog's not a deal breaker."

"I can handle a dog. As long as she's yours."

"I can handle no kids. As long as you're mine."

Khani laughed so hard it rolled through her belly in gigantic waves. She braced her hands on either side of his face, let her gaze rove over the cuffs at his ankles and wrists, and then centered on his gaze. "You're mine, King, and I'm about to show you just how much fun it can be."

PRISONER MINE
A BASE BRANCH NOVEL

Can the bad boy protect the good girl...

Zeke Slaughter played two sides against the middle and found himself in a world of hurt. Luckily, there was one person in the world who cared enough about his rogue ass to save it. But neither his sister nor the Base Branch, the UN special forces division she works for, can help him sort through the lies, money, violence, and corruption he's gotten himself into. Himself...and others. Yep, he'd dragged his team into the mix. Pin another Medal of Honor to his chest for that rookie move. Oh wait, mercenaries don't get badges of honor.

Greer Britton joined the US Elite's brand of private military to please her father, a third-generation Marine and Senate-seat legacy that failed to attain the brass of his blood before him. She doesn't want to think he sabotaged her promising career in the Marines, but... When she ends up a high-priced sex slave for the Russian mob she'd been commissioned to infiltrate with her closed-off leader, Zeke Slaughter, she questions her dad's motive for having her placed on the team.

It's up to Zeke to save his team and complete his missions without getting killed--and without crossing the line with a pristine beauty who has no business in any military, much less surrounded by a horde of violent, horny bastards...himself included.

FOR ALL TO SEE
A BUREAU NOVEL

Pristine waters and purified evil.

Two by two, dark-haired beauties vanish only to reappear as hanging, plundered corpses. The Virgin Islands boast diamond-white beaches, lush green mountains, a rich cultural heritage—and a brutal killer.

Three years on the "Field-Dresser" case and Special Agent Nathan Brewer is days away from catching the bastard—if he can convince a certain brunette to trust him. Only the woman is more likely to take a casual stroll on the surface of the sun.

After fleeing her troubles in the United States for the quiet life of a school teacher on the island of Tortola, Madelyn Garrett never imagined she'd be fixated upon by pure evil.

In a fight for her life—with a dwindling number of friends—she must rely on her cunning and Nathan's skills for survival.

VERSIONS
A BLACKLIST NOVELLA

The truth doesn't have versions. Or does it?

Rin Lee covered her childhood in dirt and danced on its grave. Only she pranced a little too hard and spent her young-adult life tiptoeing the straight and narrow. Things finally paid off in the form of a job with the Department of Defense, a home of her own, and a boyfriend muscled enough he put Zach Efron to shame. Until one text reveals a hideous truth that splinters her world.

Suddenly she can't trust Nate or their surrogate family of friends. Can she possibly trust Luck—the man who mirrors her soul, scares her beyond the neat confines she's erected around herself, and makes her scrutinize the versions she's always been too angry to see?

Luck turned to the streets out of necessity, while Rin slapped on blinders and ignored those willing to help her. A stupid move for a sultry young woman. But the skills she learned in the rough and tumble underbelly of DC will serve his latest assignment well. Because people like them have the instinct to survive.

Megan Mitcham was born and raised among the live oaks and shrimp boats of the Mississippi Gulf Coast, where her enormous family still calls home. She attended college at the University of Southern Mississippi where she received a bachelor's degree in curriculum, instruction, and special education. For several years Megan worked as a teacher in Mississippi. She married and moved to South Carolina and began working for an international non-profit organization as an instructor and co-director.

In 2009 Megan fell in love with books. Until then, books had been a source for research or the topic of tests. But one day she read *Mercy* by Julie Garwood. And oh, Mercy, she was hooked!

Megan lives in Southern Arkansas where she pens heart pounding romantic thriller novels and window-steaming erotic romance. For information on releases and giveaways subscribe at meganmitcham.com!

Facebook: @MeganMMMitcham
Twitter: MeganMitchamAuthor
Pinterest: MeganMitcham5
Goodreads: Megan_Mitcham
Website: www.meganmitcham.com

Praise for the Bureau Series

"A crime/thriller/suspense that had me gripped from beginning to end, and indeed, into book two!"

   - **Archaeolibrarian**

"Megan's writing reminds me a little of Sandra Brown & I am looking forward to reading book two in the series *Painted Walls*."

   - **Sam**, Tigerlilly Books

"Exciting, enticing, mysteriously captivating storyline kept me glued to my digital screen."

   - **5 Star Amazon Review**, For All to See

"Ms. Mitcham has written a gripping story that will keep the reader on the edge of the seat and also keep the brain actively trying to figure out whodunit. An absolutely great read!"

   - **The Sassy Bookster**

FOR INFORMATION ON NEW RELEASES & GIVEAWAYS, SIGN UP FOR MEGAN'S NEWSLETTER AT WWW.MEGANMITCHAM.COM.

Made in the USA
Lexington, KY
09 March 2016